Khan's Clerkenwell Catnapping Caper

A Jessie Harper Paranormal Cozy Mystery

KJ Cornwall

Hendry Publishing

Copyright © 2024 by Stephen Bentley

All rights reserved.

No part of this publication may be reproduced, distributed, or transmitted in any form or by any means, including photocopying, recording, or other electronic or mechanical methods, without the prior written permission of the publisher, except as permitted by U.S. copyright law. For permission requests, contact Hendry Publishing at info@hendrypublishing.com.

All characters and events in this novel – even those characters with real people's names and used with their permission – are entirely fictional. Khan is definitely fictional. The other names, all the characters, places, and incidents are a product of the author's imagination except where they are not. Place names, locales and public names are sometimes used for atmospheric purposes. Any resemblance to actual people, living or dead, or to businesses, companies, events, institutions, or locales is completely coincidental.

Book Cover by the Book Khaleesi

Contents

1. Chapter One — 1
2. Chapter Two — 25
3. Chapter Three — 45
4. Chapter Four — 60
5. Chapter Five — 72
6. Chapter Six — 94
7. Chapter Seven — 103
8. Chapter Eight — 126
9. Chapter Nine — 145
10. Chapter Ten — 167
11. Chapter Eleven — 187
12. Chapter Twelve — 205
13. Chapter Thirteen — 222
14. Chapter Fourteen — 229
15. Chapter Fifteen — 241

16. Chapter Sixteen	255
About the Author	279
Also By	282
Acknowledgements	287

Chapter One

Jessie Harper sat at her desk in the dimly lit office of Dale Street Private Investigations Agency, surrounded by towering stacks of case files. Her auburn hair was pulled back into a practical bun, and her piercing hazel eyes darted back and forth as she sifted through the papers. It was clear that her mind was hard at work, furrowed brow and all, as she searched for their next paranormal challenge.

"Another day, another pile of unsolved mysteries," she muttered with determination, fingers brushing over the worn edges of each file.

In the corner of the room stood George Jenkins, his tall stature slightly stooped as he paced back and forth with his cane. The scent of tobacco wafted through the air from the pipe clutched between his teeth, and his sharp brown eyes betrayed a restlessness that mirrored Jessie's own eagerness for a new case.

"Jessie, I'm about ready to start investigating why my tea's gone cold if we don't find something soon," George quipped, his dry humour momentarily lightening the mood.

"Patience, G.J.," Jessie replied without looking up, her lips curling into a smile. "We'll find our next case soon enough."

Her fondness for George rekindled a recent memory when they discovered they had romantic feelings for each other:

> *They had been discussing their business partnership after their last big case when Jessie had said, "—But as something more?" [than business partners] Jessie ventured, her words barely above a whisper, yet laden with hope. The question hung in the air, delicate as the porcelain teacups on the office desk.*
>
> *George exhaled a chuckle, closing the distance between them until they stood a breath apart. "Exactly. I care about you, Jessie. More than I've allowed myself to admit until now."*
>
> *Jessie felt a smile tugging at the corners of her mouth, her pulse quickening with the realisation that their connection had evolved, shaped by the trust and intimacy that grew from shared dangers and victories.*
>
> *"Life's too short for maybes," she said, meeting his gaze head-on, her own admission freeing. "I care about*

> *you too, George. And I'm willing to see where this goes—if you are."*

I, Khan, had now worked closely with Jessie Harper and George Jenkins on several mysteries involving the paranormal. I recall vividly how they reacted on the case of the murdered docker.

> *Jessie crouched beside the twisted lock, her fingers running over the rusted edges. Her brow furrowed, not in frustration, but in deep concentration. The others had given up hours ago, chalking the puzzle up to another dead end. But not Jessie. She had spent the better part of the night quietly dismantling every possibility, tracing each lead with the precision of a surgeon.*
>
> *The faintest sound of the wind slipped through the cracks of the abandoned warehouse, but Jessie barely noticed. She was close. Her fingers, dirt-streaked but steady, moved with a purpose that spoke louder than any words could. With a soft click, the lock gave way, and a rare smile tugged at the corner of her mouth.*
>
> *The others might not have noticed the faint indentation on the latch—the one hint that it hadn't been abandoned after all—but Jessie had. It wasn't about proving them wrong; it was about what was right.*

Someone needed to find the truth. She would, no matter how long it took.

Jessie stood up, dusting off her hands as her eyes scanned the shadows. Her sharp gaze missed nothing, yet it wasn't the cold calculation of a detective looking for a win. No, it was something deeper, quieter—like a moral compass that never wavered. She'd solve the mystery, not for the glory, but for the people who needed justice, even if they never knew her name.

Her breath came out slow, measured. Alone or not, she'd get to the bottom of this. She always did.

Then George Jenkins arrived at the edge of the crime scene, arms crossed, surveying the chaos. The police forensic team had been in a hurry bustling around as if speed would somehow make up for their lack of precision. He took a deep breath, eyes narrowing on the single muddy footprint everyone seemed to be stepping over. Not that they noticed.

His fingers brushed against his chin thoughtfully. "Careful, folks. That footprint might actually matter," he said, voice steady, just loud enough for the closest officer to hear. His tone wasn't accusatory—just a quiet statement of fact. The hurried shuffling paused for a moment, a few pairs of eyes glancing his way. No one protested.

George pulled out a small notebook, flipping it open as he bent down to study the print more closely. No theatrics, no rush. Each movement was deliberate, as though the scene would tell him what he needed if he just listened hard enough.

Jessie, pacing in the background, was ready to charge ahead—he could practically hear the gears turning in her head. Without looking up, George spoke. "Wait, Jessie. There's a pattern here. And if we miss it, we'll be chasing shadows all night."

She stopped mid-step, shooting him an annoyed glance, but George didn't waver. His eyes stayed fixed on the footprint, tracing its edges, already piecing together the puzzle. A flash of something crossed his face—his version of a smile—so quick it was easy to miss.

"A pound to a penny says this belongs to size nine work boots, right foot's more worn down. Heavy step on the outside edge. Left-handed, too," he said, almost absentmindedly.

Jessie raised an eyebrow, fighting a grin. "You get all that from one muddy boot print?"

George finally glanced up, deadpan. "No. I got it from two. There's another one by the door."

She shook her head, half-laughing as she turned back to the scene. George's gaze returned to his notebook, pen

> *tapping lightly on the page, his calm cutting through the noise around him. Moments later, a small smirk tugged at his lips.*

They are a good team and I am also part of that team.

Back to the office and as Jessie and George continued to search through the files, their shared determination to uncover the hidden truths of the world around them was evident. With every passing moment, their excitement grew, building towards the thrill of the chase as they prepared to dive headfirst into yet another mystery.

Perched regally on the windowsill, I observed Jessie and George with my penetrating green eyes. My sleek, black fur shimmered in the sunlight as it streamed through the glass, casting a warm glow over the room. Despite my small size, I carried myself with an air of mystery that even my magical abilities couldn't fully explain. I know I am of ancient origins and it was my good fortune that Jessie adopted me when she first saw me when she was still a librarian in Liverpool. That was quite some time ago but with the passage of time Jessie and I have developed an unbreakable bond and share the ability to communicate with each other telepathically. Becoming invisible at will is another thing you must know about me.

"Ah," George sighed, glancing up at me as he paused in his pacing, "the life of a cat must be terribly exciting, eh Khan? No tedious case files, just sunbathing and plotting world domination."

"George, you wound me," I said stretching the words like elastic and my tone filled with sarcasm. "I assure you, my days are filled with much more than plotting world domination. There's also napping, grooming, and, of course, keeping you two out of trouble."

Jessie chuckled as she looked up from her desk, her hazel eyes twinkling with amusement. "Best we don't ever dare to praise him, G.J., or we'll have a very smug feline on our hands."

"Too late for that, I'm afraid," I quipped, flicking my tail nonchalantly. "But since we're on the subject, might I suggest you humans pick up the pace in finding our next challenge? My brilliant intellect is wasted on birdwatching."

"Your wish is our command, oh wise one," Jessie said with a grin, shuffling through the case files once more. She exchanged a glance with George, who took his pipe from between his teeth and tapped it thoughtfully against his chin.

"Alright then, let's find ourselves something worth sinking our teeth into." He winked at me, and I couldn't help but smirk back.

As the three of us delved into the mysteries before us, I couldn't help but feel a sense of pride in our motley crew. For those not in the know, the crew consisted of me, Jessie, George and Detective Sergeant Bill Roberts of the Liverpool City Police, our mentor in all things to do with police investigations. Jessie had always been able to hear me and see me even when I am invisible to others. As we worked together on investigations, George also began to hear and see me when I threw on my cloak of invisibility. Then during our toughest investigation to date: the double murder at Lady Evelyn's mansion, Bill Roberts could also see and hear me.

Though we each had our own unique abilities and perspectives, together we formed a formidable team, bound by our shared pursuit of truth. And as I basked in the warm sunlight, my mind filled with the promise of adventure, I knew that whatever challenges lay ahead, we would face them head-on, side by side, humans and I.

"Ah, Jessie, I do believe we're one crossword puzzle away from joining a knitting circle," George remarked, leaning heavily on his cane as he watched her sort through the files. "I never thought I'd say this, but I'm almost desperate enough to take on a case involving a ghostly knitting needle thief."

"Careful there, George," Jessie fired back, smirking as she flipped through the papers. "You might just unravel the very fabric of our existence with that kind of talk. Besides, I know you secretly yearn for a good old-fashioned haunting now and then."

"Touché, my dear," George chuckled, raising an eyebrow at her retort. Their camaraderie was obvious making even me – a magical talking cat – feel right at home in their presence.

Just as the playful banter continued, the door to our office swung open and in strode Detective Sergeant Bill Roberts. His authoritative presence seemed to fill the room instantly, leaving no doubt as to why he was a respected Liverpool City Police detective. The lines on his face and the greying flecks in his reddish hair spoke of years spent tirelessly pursuing justice.

"Harper, Jenkins," Bill greeted them curtly, his blue eyes surveying the cluttered office as if searching for something amiss. "I hope I'm not interrupting any important discussions about the paranormal knitting underworld?"

"Never too busy for you, Bill," Jessie replied with a grin, setting aside the case files and folding her hands on the desk. "What brings you to our humble abode?"

"Time to get you to work. An urgent matter has come up in London," Bill explained, his voice taking on a more serious tone. "They've requested my assistance on a particularly peculiar case and given your expertise in the field of paranormal investigation, I thought it only fitting that you two join me."

"London, eh?" George mused, tapping his pipe thoughtfully. "Sounds like just the change of scenery we've been looking for. I thought they were the bees' knees down in the Smoke so why do they want us?"

"Can't fool you, George, can I? The truth is our old friend Lady Evelyn has recommended us to lead the investigation."

"Indeed? How wonderful!" Jessie said, her eyes lighting up with excitement. "Tell us more about this case, Bill. We're all ears... and whiskers," she added with a glance in my direction.

"Ah yes, Khan," Bill acknowledged me with a nod. "I trust your unique talents will prove invaluable as well."

"Of course," I purred, stretching languidly on the windowsill. "You know I always relish a good mystery."

"Excellent," Bill said, getting straight to the point. "A series of unexplained events has been plaguing the city and it's our job to get to the bottom of it. We leave for London first thing tomorrow morning."

"Count us in," Jessie declared, exchanging a determined look with George. "We'll pack our bags and meet you at Lime Street train station."

"Very good," Bill said. "I'll see you there."

At the prospect of a trip to the capital, Jessie and George shared a knowing smile, their excitement for the upcoming adventure evident. The prospect of a new case, filled with intrigue was exactly what they – and I – had been craving.

"Khan," Jessie began, her voice filled with anticipation, "I have a feeling this one is going to be quite the caper."

"Indeed," I concurred, my tail twitching with eagerness. "And I, for one, can't wait to unravel its mysteries."

The moment was charged with anticipation, and I watched from my perch on the windowsill as Bill continued to unfold the details of our next case. His blue eyes fixed onto Jessie and George's, commanding their full attention.

"Right," he started, his Welsh accent crisp and authoritative. "We've got a rather unusual situation on our hands. Over the past few weeks, several pedigree cats have gone missing in London. All of them belonging to wealthy families, and every one of them has received a ransom note demanding a sizeable sum for their return."

"Kidnapped kitties?" George raised an eyebrow, intrigued. "That's a new one."

Jessie leaned forward in her chair, her hazel eyes narrowed in thought. "What do the police know about the kidnappers so far?"

"Very little, I'm afraid," Bill admitted. "The ransom notes have been delivered by ragamuffins, but when they tried to trace them, the police there hit dead ends every time. It's as if these criminals have vanished into thin air. However, a Detective Inspector Ward believes the gang are from Clerkenwell.

"These catnappers sound like a slippery lot," I said, wondering if I had just coined a new word. Jessie and George glanced at me, trying to maintain their composure as they carried on the conversation with Bill.

"Are there any patterns or similarities between the victims or the cats themselves?" Jessie asked, her mind already racing through possible theories.

"Each cat is a purebred, belonging to an exclusive breed," Bill explained. "As for the families, they all seem to be part of high society – attending the same functions, frequenting the same clubs. It's clear that the kidnappers are targeting a specific clientele."

"Interesting," George mused. "And what do you want us to do?"

"Your job will be to infiltrate this upper-crust circle and gather information," Bill instructed. "We need to find out who's behind these abductions and put a stop to their scheme before any more cats – or their owners – are put in danger."

"Ah," I said, lounging leisurely on the windowsill, "A feline-focused caper for our ragtag team of investigators. How utterly delightful."

Jessie stifled a chuckle while George rolled his eyes at my comment. Bill said, "Thanks for that, Khan. We need to recover those cats and bring the culprits to justice as soon as possible."

"Count on us, Bill," George said firmly and with determination. "We won't let you down."

And so, we prepared ourselves for a new adventure – one filled with mystery, danger, and perhaps even a bit of humour courtesy of yours truly, Khan, the enigmatic feline.

The sun was now casting long shadows across the room as Jessie, George, and Bill stood around the desk, discussing their strategy for the upcoming investigation in London. I observed from my perch on the windowsill, tail flicking lazily.

"Right," George began, leaning on his cane as he looked over copies of the ransom notes sent to Bill Roberts by the London police. "We'll head to London first thing tomorrow morning. We'll need to visit the families of the kidnapped cats and gather any information we can."

"Sounds like a plan," Jessie agreed. She scribbled down a few notes, her auburn hair catching stray beams of sunlight. "

"Isn't it marvellous how we always find ourselves in the most curious of predicaments?" I said, "one moment we're solving a case involving a haunted mansion and murders and the next, we're tracking down conniving catnappers!"

"Speaking of which," Jessie said with a wistful smile, clearly reminiscing about one of our past cases, "remember the time we went undercover at that séance? George, you made quite an impression as the eccentric medium!"

"Ah, yes!" George chuckled, his eyes twinkling with amusement. "That was rather entertaining, wasn't it? We exposed the fraud behind the so-called 'spirits' and helped put an end to that charlatan's career."

"Indeed," I purred, pleased with the shared memory. "It was during that very case when our partnership truly solidified. We've come a long way since then, my dear friends."

Jessie nodded, her eyes softening for a moment. "We have, and I wouldn't trade our adventures for anything."

"Nor would I," George agreed, his voice filled with warmth and affection.

"Let's not get too sentimental now," Bill interjected, bringing them back to the task at hand. "We've got a case to solve, and those cats won't rescue themselves."

"Of course, Bill," Jessie said, shaking off the nostalgia and refocusing on their plan. "We'll make sure we're prepared for anything that comes our way in London."

"Excellent," Bill replied, satisfied with their determination. "I have no doubt that you two –" He paused, glancing briefly at me before continuing, "and our…unusual feline companion will be more than up to the challenge."

"Rest assured, Detective Sergeant," I purred smugly, basking in the praise. "With our combined skills and expertise, no catnapper can hope to elude us for long."

As the sun vanished entirely, leaving only the office lights to illuminate the room, Jessie, George, and Bill continued to discuss their plans for the investigation in London. Despite the uncertainty and danger that lay ahead, there was no denying the excitement that thrummed through each of us, eager as ever to tackle yet another thrilling mystery.

One of the lights flickered casting wavering shadows on the office walls as Jessie, George, and Bill concluded their discussion. I lounged atop a towering stack of books, tail swishing lazily as I took in the scene before me.

"Right then," Jessie declared, her eyes sparkling. "We're off to London first thing tomorrow morning. We'll need to pack light and be prepared for anything."

"Indeed," George agreed, absentmindedly tapping his cane on the floor. "I'll make sure we have all the necessary supplies and equipment ready to go."

"Excellent," Bill chimed in, an authoritative air about him. "I'll notify my superiors here and in London you'll be assisting us on this case. I'm certain they'll be most grateful for your involvement."

"Speaking of involvement, how do you plan on keeping me out of sight while we're there?" I asked, raising an eyebrow. "I may be able to make myself invisible to most humans, but at other times it's not as though I can simply stroll through the streets without attracting attention."

"Leave that to me, Khan," Jessie replied, a mischievous glint in her eye. "I've got a few tricks up my sleeve when it comes to disguises."

"Disguises?" I muttered dubiously, but any further protests were drowned out by George's hearty laughter.

"Have faith, Khan," he said, still chuckling. "Jessie's creativity has gotten us out of more than one tight spot over the years."

"True enough," I conceded, recalling numerous adventures where Jessie's quick thinking had saved the day. "Very well, I shall trust in your ingenuity."

"Thank you, Khan," Jessie said, shooting me a warm smile. "Now, let's get some rest. Tomorrow is going to be a long day."

"Indeed," George agreed, stifling a yawn as he gathered up his cane and pipe. "Sleep well, everyone. We've got a big day ahead of us."

Isabel, the receptionist, had long gone home so Jessie turned off the lights plunging the room into darkness, save for the soft glow of moonlight filtering through the window. I could feel the anticipation building within me, a familiar thrill that accompanied the start of each new case.

"Goodnight, Jessie," I whispered as she headed towards her bedroom.

"Goodnight, Khan," she replied softly, pausing at the door to share one last, excited grin with me before she gave George a goodnight kiss before he entered his separate bedroom.

"Goodnight, George," I called out to him, receiving only a muffled grunt in response. But I knew, beneath his gruff exterior, he was just as eager as we were to dive headfirst into our latest adventure.

As sleep slowly overcame me, I couldn't help but wonder what awaited us in London. What challenges would we face? What secrets would be uncovered? And most importantly, could we succeed in rescuing those precious felines from their kidnappers?

Only time would tell, but one thing was certain: Jessie Harper, George Jenkins, and I – Khan, the magical, talking cat – were ready to take on whatever lay ahead, together.

THE MORNING SUN FILTERED through the window casting a warm golden glow across the room as I stretched my legs and yawned, feeling the last remnants of sleep dissipate from my body. Jessie was already up and about, her swift footsteps echoing faintly from the hallway. The scent of freshly brewed coffee wafted in the air, mingling with the aroma of buttered toast.

"Khan, breakfast is ready!" Jessie called out, her voice cheerful and energetic.

"Coming!" I replied, my stomach rumbling in anticipation. I leapt gracefully from the windowsill, landing softly on the wooden floor before padding towards the kitchen area that also served as the dining room.

"Morning, old chap," George greeted me, his eyes sparkling with excitement as he took a sip of his steaming coffee. He looked refreshed and eager to start the day, his cane propped against the table and his pipe resting unlit in his jacket pocket.

"Good morning, George." I nodded, settling into my usual spot by the fireplace. Jessie slid a plate of scrambled eggs and smoked salmon in front of me, a treat reserved for special occasions – or the start of a new case.

"Thank you, Jessie," I said gratefully, tucking into my meal with gusto. "I'm going to need all the energy I can get for our trip to London."

"Quite right, Khan," she agreed, smiling as she bit into her own slice of toast. "We'll be catching the late morning train, so we have just enough time to pack and make any necessary preparations."

"Speaking of which," George interjected, leaning back in his chair and tapping his fingers thoughtfully on the tabletop. "Do we have any contacts in London who might be able to assist us?"

Jessie's brow furrowed as she pondered the question. "Well, not really. We have no option but to rely on Detective Inspector Clement Ward who Bill mentioned."

"Ah, yes," George said, nodding in recognition. "You're right. I do hear he's a good man. A bit of a stickler for protocol, but his heart's in the right place."

"Perhaps it would be wise to send him a telegram ahead of our arrival," I suggested between bites of egg. "It might smooth our path and ensure we have access to any resources we might need."

"Capital idea, Khan!" Jessie exclaimed, her eyes lighting up with enthusiasm. "I'll send one off right away, once we've finished breakfast."

As we continued our meal, discussing the logistics of our upcoming journey, I couldn't help but feel a tingling sensation of anticipation coursing through my veins. London held so many possibilities, so many secrets waiting to be uncovered. And with Jessie and George by my side, there was no doubt in my mind that we were more than capable of rising to the challenge.

"Here's to a successful case," I toasted, raising an imaginary glass of champagne in the air.

"Cheers to that!" Jessie and George chimed in unison, their laughter filling the room as we braced ourselves for the adventure that lay ahead.

The train's rhythmic chug-chug-chugging provided a comforting soundtrack as we settled into our first-class compartment, bound for London. I sat perched atop the plush seat, my tail swishing languidly, while Jessie and George sorted through their luggage, stowing it neatly in the overhead racks. Poor old Bill Roberts was sat alone in a second-class compartment miffed that the force would not permit him to travel first-class.

"Khan, do you think Ward received our telegram?" Jessie asked, her brow furrowed with concern as she fiddled with her hatpin.

"Telegrams are generally quite reliable," I reassured her, flicking an imaginary speck of dust from my immaculate fur. "I'm certain he'll be prepared for our arrival."

"Besides," George chimed in, leaning on his cane and winking at me, "if he didn't receive it, we'll make sure to give him the shock of his life when we show up unannounced at Scotland Yard."

"Ah, yes, nothing like a little spontaneous chaos to keep things interesting," I mused, a grin tugging at my whiskers. "I've always admired your ability to stir the pot, George."

"Thank you, Khan," George replied, clearly pleased by my observation. "I do try my best."

Jessie shook her head, a fond smile playing on her lips. "You two will be the death of me someday, I swear."

"Only after we've solved this case, dear Jessie," I said, batting my emerald eyes innocently. "We wouldn't dream of leaving you in the lurch in this life nor the hereafter as you humans are wont to call it."

"Speaking of the case," George added, "it might be a good time to go over some of our strategies before we reach London. We don't want to arrive unprepared."

"Agreed," Jessie nodded, her expression turning serious. "Let's start with what we know about the kidnapped cats and the ransom demands."

As the three of us delved into the details of the case, I reflected on the partnership. Jessie's keen instincts and tireless pursuit of justice balanced perfectly with George's methodical approach and dry humour. And as for me, well, my magical abilities and feline cunning added an extra layer of unpredictability that kept even the most seasoned criminals on their toes.

"Jessie, I think it's important to note that all the kidnapped cats are pedigrees," George pointed out, tapping his cane thoughtfully against the carpeted floor. "It suggests that the kidnapper is specifically targeting valuable animals."

"True," Jessie mused, her hazel eyes narrowing in concentration. "And the ransom demands, while exorbitant, do seem to be proportional to the cats' worth. It could indicate that our culprit is motivated by financial gain rather than some twisted form of revenge or cruelty."

"An excellent point," I agreed. "It appears our perpetrator is driven purely by profit, hence the targeting of wealthy owners exclusively."

"Indeed," George concurred, stroking his chin thoughtfully. "There must be some other factor at play here, something we haven't yet uncovered."

"Let's not get too far ahead of ourselves," Jessie cautioned, holding up a hand to forestall further speculation. "We'll have more information once we speak with DI Ward and examine the crime scenes firsthand."

"Patience, Jessie?" I teased, arching an eyebrow in mock surprise. "Now there's a virtue I never thought I'd see you embrace."

"Very funny, Khan," she retorted, rolling her eyes good-naturedly. "Now, let's focus on our plan for when we arrive in London."

As we continued our discussion, the train sped along the tracks with its continuous clickety-clacking bringing us ever closer to the heart of the mystery that awaited us.

Chapter Two

THE DIM GLOW OF a single lamp illuminated the small office at New Scotland Yard, casting shadows across the stacks of papers and well-worn maps that covered the desk. Jessie Harper leaned forward; her eyes alight with an inner glow as she spoke in hushed tones to George. I perched atop a dusty filing cabinet, my green eyes flicking back and forth between them, taking in every word and nuance.

"George, this catnapping case is unlike anything we've ever encountered," Jessie whispered urgently. "We have to take it on. If we can crack this, it'll cement our reputation as the foremost investigators in England."

"Agreed," George replied, his eyes glinting in the lamplight as he tapped his pipe thoughtfully against his cane. "But we need a solid strategy. This isn't Liverpool – London's criminal underworld is an entirely different beast."

"True," Jessie conceded, absently twisting a stray strand of hair around her finger. "Better safe than sorry, after all. Let's go over everything we brought with us for the investigation."

They began cataloguing their arsenal – a mix of conventional tools like magnifying glasses and fingerprint powder, along with more specialized items such as enchanted talismans and ancient scrolls.

I couldn't help but smile inwardly, impressed by their attention to detail and preparedness. Their excitement was contagious and my tail twitched with anticipation as I made mental notes of their inventory.

"Alright," Jessie said, "We've got everything we need. Now, let's discuss how we're going to approach this investigation."

"First things first, I believe we need to establish a base of operations in Clerkenwell," George suggested. "Somewhere inconspicuous, where we can keep an eye on the comings and goings of the locals."

"Right," Jessie agreed. "And we'll need to start by interviewing the socialites who reported the kidnappings. They might have valuable information about the other victims."

"Excellent point," George nodded. "From there, we can begin piecing together the connections between the cases and unravel the mystery behind this catnapping ring."

I leapt down from my perch to join them, stretching languidly before curling up at Jessie's feet. They were a formidable trio, my companions – their determination and ingenuity never failed to impress me. I couldn't help but sense a thrill of excitement at the possibility of tackling yet another strange and perilous case with them.

As Jessie, George and Bill Roberts were discussing strategies, the door to the office swung open with a sudden force that made me flinch. A tall man with salt-and-pepper hair strode into the room, his piercing gaze and air of authority making it clear he was someone not to be trifled with. I made myself invisible.

"Detective Inspector Clement Ward," he announced, his voice booming through the small space. "Clerkenwell police division."

"Ah, DI Ward," Bill said, extending his hand in greeting. "I've heard quite a bit about you. I'm DS Bill Roberts seconded from Liverpool City Police and this is Jessie Harper and George Jenkins of Liverpool's Dale Street Private Investigations Agency."

"Charmed, I'm sure," Jessie replied dryly, her eyes narrowing ever so slightly as she assessed the newcomer. George merely nodded, his sharp eyes studying the detective inspector intently.

"Inspector," Bill began, adopting a more serious tone. "We're here because of the recent string of catnappings. The Dale Street Private Investigations Agency has been called in to assist. Time is of the essence, and we need everyone's efforts to solve this case."

"Of course," Ward said, his expression unreadable. "But I hope you understand that my team and I have our own methods. We won't hesitate to make tough decisions if it means cracking this case. And remember this, you are only here because Lady Pandora Street-Walters, asked for you after her Mr Whiskers went missing."

"She did?" Jessie said looking puzzled.

"You were recommended to her by Lady Evelyn Montague. I believe you are familiar with her?" Ward said.

"Indeed," George said.

"Understood, sir," Bill said, his voice measured. "But we also have our own unique skills and expertise. We must work together if we want the best chance at success."

"Indeed," Jessie said, a hint of defiance in her voice. "We didn't come all the way from Liverpool just to watch from the sidelines. We fully intend to be involved in every aspect of this investigation."

"Very well," Ward sighed, seemingly resigned to the inevitable clash of approaches. "Just remember, this isn't some game. These kidnappings have caused an uproar in the city and it's our job to restore order."

"Trust me, Inspector," Jessie said, her tone unwavering. "We're well aware of the stakes. And we'll do whatever it takes to make sure the catnappers are arrested."

As I watched the exchange unfold before me, my whiskers twitched with a mix of tension and anticipation. It was clear that we were all venturing into uncharted territory and only time would tell if this uneasy alliance would yield the results we so desperately needed.

"Right, no time to waste," Bill Roberts said briskly, his voice cutting through the lingering tension in the office. "We need to get moving on this case."

Jessie and George shared a surprised glance before springing into action, their eagerness to begin was obvious. Jessie quickly gathered her leather satchel, ensuring she had everything she needed for their investigation, while George grabbed his homburg hat and cane.

"Let's go," Jessie said, her eyes sparkling as she adjusted the strap of her satchel.

"Yes, right-oh," George replied, placing his hat securely on his head as he leaned on his cane. "We have no time to dilly dally."

As the humans left the Scotland Yard office, I darted after them still invisible to all except for my colleagues and of course I include Bill. My tail was swishing with anticipation. Our borrowed police car awaited us outside. Its polished black paint gleamed in the midday sun. As our police driver slid behind the wheel, George settled into the front passenger seat and Bill and Jessie climbed into the back. I leapt onto the dashboard, taking my rightful place as an observer of all things mysterious.

Safe in the knowledge Jessie and I can communicate telepathically at my behest, I heard, "Alright, Khan." Jessie spoke my name with a grin, her fingers drumming on the window. "Let's see what London has in store for us."

As we drove through the streets of central London towards Clerkenwell, the city buzzed around us like a hive of activity. Horse-drawn carriages and cars competed for space on the streets, a cacophony of horns and hooves filling the air. My whiskers quivered, reacting to the assault of sounds and scents that crowded my senses, but I was determined to keep my focus on the task at hand.

"Bill, you mentioned earlier that there have been several other catnappings," George said from the passenger seat glancing at the passing buildings. "What can you tell us about those cases?"

"Not much to add, really... let me see... five cats have gone missing in the last month alone," Bill replied, his voice sombre. "Most from wealthy families, and all with ransom demands but no indication of where they might be or who is behind the crimes."

"Curious," Jessie said as our police driver navigated a sharp turn with ease. "It's clear that whoever is behind this has a specific motive in mind, but what could it be?"

"Perhaps they have a vendetta against the upper class?" George suggested, stroking his chin thoughtfully.

"Money," Bill said.

"Or maybe they're using the cats for some sort of supernatural purpose," I thought aloud. My ears flicked back and forth as I contemplated the possibilities. Our driver was oblivious to my presence and unable to hear a word I said. I did sense he was now heading back towards central London.

With my magical abilities switched on, our conversation flowed seamlessly as we continued to drive through London. Bill, Jessie, George and I offering our own theories and insights into the mysterious catnappings. "Whatever their motives may be," Jessie said firmly as we pulled up to our first destination, "we'll get to the bottom of this, together."

"Agreed," George echoed, his gaze meeting mine as we prepared to step out into the heart of London and begin our investigation.

"Ah, Miss Harper, Mr Jenkins, and Sergeant Roberts," said Lady Penelope Worthington as we entered her opulent drawing room on the ground floor of her Mayfair townhouse. The scent of fresh roses filled the air. Sunlight streamed through the tall windows casting a warm glow on the polished surfaces of the antique furniture.

"Thank you for seeing us, Lady Worthington," Jessie said offering a polite smile. "We understand that this must be a difficult time for you."

The socialite dismissed her butler with a wave of the hand before speaking. "Indeed, it is," she sighed, dabbing at her eyes with a silk handkerchief. "My poor Fluffy has been gone for over a week now, and I fear the worst."

"Please, tell us everything you can about the day Fluffy went missing," George urged, his voice gentle yet insistent.

"Of course," Lady Worthington began, taking a deep breath to steady herself. "It was a Tuesday morning, and my maid, Eliza, had just taken Fluffy out to the gardens for his daily stroll. She turned her back for only a moment, and when she looked again, he was gone."

"I'm assuming you are saying Fluffy was on a leash?" Jessie said.

"Oh, yes, he's terribly valuable, you see? Eliza might let him off so he can tinkle in the bushes. Apart from that, he is always in sight."

"You say valuable. Why?" George said.

"He is purebred Persian and has won prizes at shows but he is far more valuable to me as a friend, I terribly miss him so," Lady Worthington said sniffling into her handkerchief.

"Did anyone see anything unusual around that time?" Bill inquired, his piercing blue eyes searching Lady Worthington's face for any hint of a clue.

"Eliza said she saw a man wearing a dark coat and hat leaving the garden at the back gate leading onto the common but she couldn't be sure it was him," she replied, her voice trembling slightly. "I can't help but think that whoever took Fluffy might have been watching us for some time."

"Have you heard of any other similar incidents in the area?" Jessie asked, her hazel eyes narrowing as she considered the possible connections.

"Several of my friends have also lost their beloved pets," Lady Worthington confided, her expression grave. "Like me, they have received ransom demands and no word of their whereabouts."

"How much was the ransom demand?" George said.

"One thousand pounds for Fluffy's safe return," Lady Worthington said.

"How was it delivered?" Jessie asked.

"Some street urchin delivered the note by hand but ran off and disappeared," the socialite said.

"Any contact from the kidnappers since then?" Bill said.

"Nothing."

"They will be in touch, I'm sure of that and when they are, it's imperative you let us know," Bill said.

"We'll do our best to find Fluffy and the other missing cats, Lady Worthington," Jessie assured her. "You have our word."

"Thank you," she whispered, her eyes filling with tears once more.

As we left the Worthington townhouse, I could sense the urgency and determination emanating from Jessie,

George, and Bill. They were acutely aware of the pressure to solve this mystery.

"Time is of the essence," Bill declared as we climbed back into the borrowed police car. "We need to start piecing together any clues or leads we can find."

"Agreed," George said. "We should look into any connections between the victims and see if there's a pattern."

"Let's also speak with some of the locals," Jessie said, her voice firm. "Someone must have seen or heard something that could lead us in the right direction."

"Alright then," Bill nodded as the police driver started the engine. "Let's get to work."

As we drove off, my whiskers twitched with anticipation. The game was afoot and I hoped that with Jessie, George, and Bill on the case, it wouldn't be long before the truth was revealed.

By prior arrangement we made our way to Clerkenwell police station where we again met Detective Inspector Clement Ward. He was waiting for us in the cramped CID office. Leaning against the wall with his hands clasped behind his back, he surveyed the room with a keen eye that seemed to miss nothing.

"Ah, good to see you're back," Clement said, his deep voice filled with authority. "I've been looking into London's criminal underworld and I have a plan for our investigation."

Jessie and George exchanged curious glances as we gathered around the large table, where a map of London was spread out before us.

"Through my map-making contacts, I've managed to narrow down a few locations where these catnappings have been taking place," Ward explained, pointing to several spots on the map including Mayfair, Westminster and Kensington. "It seems they're targeting wealthy neighbourhoods, which makes sense if they're hoping for a quick and lucrative payout."

"Interesting," Jessie said, her brow furrowed in thought. "But how do we narrow it down further? There are still so many possibilities."

"Patience, Miss Harper," Ward replied with a slight smile. "My detectives will start by conducting surveillance on these areas and interviewing any potential witnesses. And speaking of witnesses, I've arranged a meeting with an informant who might have some valuable information for us."

"An informant?" George asked, raising an eyebrow. "You trust this person?"

"Trust is a strong word, Mr Jenkins," Ward admitted. "But I'm confident they'll provide useful intelligence. After all, it's not their first time helping me."

As Ward spoke, I noticed the change in Jessie and George's demeanour. It was clear that, despite their initial reservations about working with him, they were beginning to recognize his expertise and experience. They shared the same look of mutual understanding and nodded in agreement.

"Alright, let's get started," Jessie said, "no time to waste and we need to get to the bottom of this as soon as possible."

"Too right," chimed in George, rolling up his sleeves. "We're ready to delve deeper into this investigation, and with your guidance, Inspector Ward, I believe we stand a solid chance of solving this mystery."

"Good," Ward replied, "Then let's crack on with it. We have work to do."

As we prepared to leave the conference room, a sense of excitement grew inside me. With Jessie, George, Bill, and now Inspector Ward on the case, it must only be a matter of time before we uncovered the truth behind these catnappings. My tail flicked back and forth – a sign of my eagerness to witness the events that were about to unfold.

As we stepped out onto the bustling streets of Clerkenwell, I couldn't help but notice a peculiar glint in Inspector Ward's eye. He led us through an increasingly labyrinthine series of alleyways, old stone walls looming on either side. Jessie, George, and Bill followed closely behind him, their curiosity piqued by the mysterious path he was taking us down.

"Inspector Ward," Jessie called out, her voice echoing slightly off the narrow walls. "Where exactly are you taking us?"

"Patience, Miss Harper," he replied, not breaking stride. "This is just a precautionary measure to ensure our investigation remains covert."

"Covert?" George inquired, his interest visibly growing. "What exactly have you got planned for us, Inspector?"

"Ah, you'll see soon enough," Ward said with a cryptic smile. "Trust me when I say it will be worth the wait."

Bill grumbled under his breath, obviously not as thrilled about the secrecy as the rest of us.

As we continued to navigate the intricate network of alleyways resembling a Dickensian scene, I couldn't help but experience a mixture of anticipation and unease. What challenges would we face in this city that required such discretion? And how would we overcome them?

"Here we are," announced Ward, stopping abruptly at a nondescript door hidden within the shadows of the alley. He rapped sharply on the surface and after a moment, the door creaked open to reveal a dimly lit room beyond.

"Welcome," he gestured for us to enter. "To the heart of London's criminal underworld. A world run by Ronnie and Reggie Blackwell. You don't want to cross them twins, believe me."

"Underworld?" Jessie whispered, her eyes wide with surprise. "You mean... we're going undercover?"

"Indeed," confirmed Ward, a mischievous glint in his eye. "And not just any undercover operation. This one requires all of us – including you, Khan – to take on new identities and infiltrate the very heart of this catnapping ring."

Why is he talking to me? I thought. Jessie came to my aid.

"Who is Khan?" Jessie said.

"Come on, Miss Harper, you can fool some but not me. I'm the wiliest detective you have ever met, no offence to you Bill."

"What on earth do you mean?" George said because Bill was flabbergasted and lost for words.

"I did background checks including a long conversation with your friend Lady Evelyn. She's not stupid, you know, she knew all along about Khan or rather she suspected he was no ordinary cat," Ward said.

I thought a while and broke the uneasy silence when I said, "Oh, well, the cat's out of the bag."

Everyone broke into a raucous laughter born more out of an easing of tension rather than what I said... though it was quite funny.

I continued, "New identities?" My tail twitched with excitement. "Now that sounds intriguing."

"Are you sure this is necessary, Inspector?" Bill asked sceptically, clearly not as enamoured with the idea as the rest of us.

"Absolutely," Ward replied firmly. "It's the only way we'll get close enough to gather the information we need without alerting them to our presence."

As we hesitated at the threshold, I could perceive the anticipation building in the air. This was it – the moment when we would dive headfirst into London's seedy underbelly taking on new personas and facing unknown dangers in our quest to solve the mystery of the catnappings. The challenge laid before us was undeniably thrilling and I couldn't wait to see how we would rise to meet it.

"Alright," Jessie finally agreed, her eyes bright and full of life, "Let's do this."

"Very well," George added, his voice steady and resolute. "For the sake of those poor cats, we'll play your game, Inspector."

"Excellent," Ward said with a smile. "Welcome to the underworld, my friends. Let the games begin."

And with that, we crossed the threshold into a dimly lit room, unsure of what lay ahead but determined to face whatever challenges London had in store for us. As the door creaked shut behind us, sealing our fate, I couldn't help but wonder: what secrets would we uncover in this dark world? And more importantly, would we ever be the same once we emerged?

But there was no turning back now. The investigation was underway, and the lives of countless innocent cats hung in the balance. It was up to us to unravel the mystery, even if it meant venturing into the heart of darkness itself.

The dimly lit room led out onto another alleyway. A chilling wind whipped between the solid, dark grey walls draped in moss as we stood in the shadows, our gazes fixed upon a dimly lit pub. I watched Jessie, George and Bill. They looked uneasy and I swear I could hear their nerves jangling beneath their calm exteriors. Ward had slipped away unnoticed so I assumed he was known as a policeman in this seemingly nefarious area of Clerkenwell.

"Remember, we need to blend in," Jessie murmured, her eyes glued to the surrounding streets. "We can't afford to draw attention to ourselves."

"Agreed," George said, gripping his cane tightly. "But let's not forget, we're here for a reason: to gather information."

"Information, right." Jessie nodded, determination set in her expression.

"Relax, you two. It's just a pub," I said, my tail flicking impatiently. "How hard could it be?"

"Easy for you to say," George retorted, his eyes glaring at me. "You can just slip in unnoticed."

"True, but I expect you both to hold your own. I grinned slyly sensing the excitement of the chase intensify within me. "Now, let's get moving. "

As we approached the entrance, I saw Jessie's hand trembling slightly. She caught my gaze and gave me a weak smile. "Here goes nothing," she whispered, pushing open the door.

The moment we stepped inside, the overpowering smell of stale beer and smoke assaulted our senses. The dimly lit room was filled with rough-looking patrons, their eyes darting towards us with suspicion.

"Act natural," Jessie muttered under her breath, forcing a casual smile.

"Right," George agreed, his posture rigid as he glanced around the room.

"Table near the back?" Jessie suggested, subtly nodding in that direction.

"Perfect," George replied, and we began weaving our way through the crowd.

"Excuse me, mates," a gruff voice called out as we neared the table. Jessie and George froze, their eyes meeting the hardened gaze of a burly man. "You lot new 'round 'ere?" He said in a Cockney accent.

"Y-yes," Jessie stammered, her cheeks flushing. "Just passing through."

"Ah, I see." The man studied us for a moment, his eyes lingering on George's cane. "Well, enjoy your drinks. But remember, we don't take kindly to outsiders pokin' their noses where they don't belong."

"Understood," George said, his voice steady despite situation, "thank you."

"Cheers," the man grunted before turning away.

Under my cloak of invisibility, I whispered, "Close call," as we finally settled at our table. "But well handled. Now, let's get to work."

"Right," Jessie agreed, her eyes scanning the room. "We need to find someone who knows something about these catnappings."

"Exactly," George said. "But we must be discreet. We don't want to raise any more suspicion than necessary."

"Leave it to me," I said, experiencing a familiar excitement bubbling within me. "I'll make my way around the pub and see what I can find out. Just act natural and try not to worry too much."

"Be careful, Khan," Jessie warned, her hazel eyes clouded with concern.

"Always am," I replied, winking before slipping away into the shadows.

As I moved covertly and invisibly through the crowd, I felt a rush of exhilaration at the challenge that was in store. This was what we did at the Dale Street Private Investigations Agency – to uncover the truth and bring justice to those in need. And with Jessie, George, Bill, myself and now DI Ward working together, there was nothing we couldn't handle.

"Bring on the underworld," I thought, my green eyes gleaming. I was itching for action.

Chapter Three

THE NEXT MORNING

I soon discovered the action would have to wait for a while. Bill Roberts called a meeting at the lodging house we were all accommodated in. A pleasant three-storey house in Vauxhall just across the Thames from Scotland Yard. It was run by an even more pleasant lady called Mrs Swarbrick who didn't mind cats and treated me as Jessie's pet, so I was always visible to Mrs B.

DS Roberts laid down the law or at least his version of it and it contradicted what DI Ward had arranged. Was this the start of inter-force jealousies, I wondered. Bill was determined to do things his way and wished to start by interviewing more of the stolen cats' owners. Bill didn't say but I suspected he didn't like the prospect of going undercover in a seedy part of London very appealing... and neither did I despite the prospect of some excitement. The encounter with the burly ruffian in the pub had been scary.

We had taken a taxi to Mayfair rather than use our designated police driver. Bill did this deliberately so Ward wouldn't know where we were or what we were up to. The Mayfair street was a testament to opulence and wealth and Jessie couldn't help but gawk at the row of grand townhouses as they approached their destination. Alighting from the taxi, George's steady cane tap provided a rhythmic counterpoint to Jessie's rapid heartbeat. Bill, ever vigilant, kept his eyes peeled for anything unusual.

"Here we are," Jessie said, as we stopped in front of a particularly lavish mansion. The intricate ironwork gate creaked open at their arrival revealing an immaculate private garden that seemed to defy the chaos of London. They strode up the marble steps and knocked on the gleaming brass door knocker. It was then I made myself invisible.

"Good afternoon," said Lady Pandora Street-Walters as she greeted them, her eyes red-rimmed from crying. "Please, come in." She led Jessie, George, and Bill Roberts into her elegant drawing room so I followed. The click of her heels echoed against the hardwood floor. Her voice trembled as she recounted the harrowing ordeal of her beloved pet's abduction. "He's gone... my precious cat, Mr Whiskers."

Jessie glanced at George as he listened carefully to the distraught woman. Bill cleared his throat, his authoritative presence calming the room. "We're here to help, ma'am," he reassured her, "and we will do everything in our power to find your cat and bring him back safely."

"Thank you," she whispered through her tears, dabbing at her eyes with a delicate handkerchief. "I don't know what I would do without him. I have every confidence in you. My friend Lady Evelyn speaks highly of you all and that is why I telephoned the Commissioner to insist you came down from Liverpool to lead the investigation."

"Why us?" Jessie said, "our speciality is with paranormal aspects of a case. Are there any such otherworldly matters connected to the kidnapping of Mr Whiskers?"

"No, dear, not that I know of. But Evelyn told me all about your professionalism and investigative skills."

"Thank you for asking for us. As we say, we will do our utmost to bring Mr Whiskers home safe and sound," Jessie said. "Now, about the kidnapping."

As the socialite continued to share the details of the kidnapping, Jessie found herself growing more invested in this case. Her heart ached for the woman in front of her, and she silently vowed to reunite her with her beloved cat.

"Have there been any other similar incidents in the area?" George asked.

"Y-yes, according to the police," the socialite replied, her voice cracking as she tried to recall the names of other wealthy individuals who had experienced similar cat kidnappings. "The police said they're all connected to high society... it's as if someone is targeting us."

That news coming from such a prominent well-to-do member of society sent a shiver down Jessie's spine and she exchanged uneasy glances with George and Bill. This confirmed they were dealing with something much bigger than a simple kidnapping – they had stumbled upon a potential catnapping ring preying on affluent pet owners.

As I watched from my perch on the grand staircase, Jessie's determined gaze never wavered from the distraught socialite. "Can you tell us exactly when and where you last saw your cat?" she asked, her voice steady and comforting.

"Y-yes," the woman stammered, wiping away fresh tears with a trembling hand. "It was two days ago, in the morning. I let him out into the garden for a little while, as I always do. When I went to bring him back inside, he was gone."

"Did you notice anything unusual or suspicious leading up to the kidnapping? Any strangers lurking around the property, or perhaps someone who seemed overly interested in your cat?" Jessie pressed gently, her keen mind working through the details of the case.

The socialite hesitated, wringing her hands anxiously. "Well, there was a man... I saw him walking by the house several times over the past week. He would always pause at the gate and peer inside as if he were looking for something."

"Could you describe this man?" George interjected, his mind zeroing in on the socialite's every word.

"Um, he was tall, with dark hair and a thin moustache," she recalled, her voice growing more confident. "He wore a dark coat and a hat pulled down so it obscured his face. I didn't think much of it at the time, but now..."

"Interesting," George murmured, taking note of the description. "And what about the ransom demand? Can you tell us anything about the contents or how you received it?"

"Of course," she replied, "the police have the note. "It was a crumpled piece of paper in a dirty envelope. It arrived in the mail yesterday along with a small lock of my cat's fur." Her voice broke as she discussed the note. "They're demanding one thousand pounds for his safe return."

"Thank you," Jessie said softly, making a mental note to later look at the ransom note. "We'll do everything we can to find your cat and bring him home safely."

I could see the gears turning in George's mind as he watched Jessie interview Lady Pandora Street-Walters. His focus was sharp, searching for any inconsistencies or hidden clues that might lead them closer to the truth. It was clear that they would need to work quickly if they were to have any hope of solving this case.

As I leapt from the staircase and padded silently towards my companions, I sensed a burning desire to see justice served. This catnapping ring had gone on long enough, and it was high time someone put a stop to it.

Lady Street-Walters' eyes brimmed with tears as she clutched a framed photograph of her beloved cat. "I've had him since he was a kitten, you see," she managed to say, her voice trembling with emotion. "He's been my constant companion for years now. I don't know what I'd do without him."

"Understandable," George said softly trying to offer some comfort. However, it was Bill who stepped in, his no-nonsense demeanour and authoritative presence calming the room.

"Ma'am, we're here to help you," Bill said, his Welsh accent steady and reassuring. "Now, let's focus on gathering all the information we can. Have you noticed any suspicious characters hanging around your home or anyone who might have a reason to target you? Other than the man you already mentioned."

She shook her head, her lips quivering. "No, I can't think of anyone who would want to hurt me or my precious cat. But there was something odd that happened a few days before the kidnapping. A man came by asking about my cat, claiming to be from a cat food company looking for models. But when I called the company, they said they didn't have anyone by that name working for them."

"Interesting," Bill said making a mental note of this potential lead. "Did you get a good look at him? Can you describe his appearance?"

As she recounted the details of the stranger, I could see Bill's mind working, analysing every piece of information. He nodded thoughtfully, jotting down notes in his small notebook.

"Thank you," Bill said, closing his notebook with a snap. "We'll need to follow up on this lead. Rest assured, we'll do everything in our power to find your cat and bring him back to you safely."

Her eyes welled up with gratitude as she dabbed at her tears with a handkerchief. "Thank you so much, all of you. I don't know what I would do without your help."

"Think nothing of it, Ma'am," Bill replied, his tone gentle but firm. "We must see justice served and ensure the safety of those in need."

The socialite's eyes widened as she clutched her handkerchief tightly. "It is shocking that my poor Mr Whiskers isn't the only one."

"Unfortunately, that seems to be the case," George chimed in, his gaze never leaving her face. "This could well be an organized catnapping ring targeting wealthy pet owners."

"Good heavens!" she gasped, her distress evident in her trembling voice. "Who else has been affected? Do I know them?"

"Lord and Lady Featherstone, for starters," Bill said, his voice sharp and steady. The room seemed to still as he spoke, a heavy silence following each word, like everyone had instinctively straightened their posture, as if the very air had thickened with unspoken consequence. "They lost their beloved Siamese just last week. And then there's Lady Penelope Worthington, the shipping magnate – her Persian disappeared about a week ago."

"Goodness, she is married to Sir Percy Worthington, the General, you know." the socialite whispered, her fingers nervously twisting at the edge of her handkerchief. "I know them both. We belong to the same clubs and attend the same charity events... Is nothing sacred anymore?"

"Apparently not," George said.

"Catnappers preying on the high society," Jessie said. "It's despicable."

"Yes, indeed, is that a word?" The socialite said.

"Beg your pardon, Ma'am. Is what a word?" George said.

"Catnappers."

I resisted the urge to say something like "it is now," but I let George answer.

"Apparently, Ma'am," George said on cue.

WITH THAT, WE TOOK our leave from the socialite's residence, our minds buzzing with the new information and the challenges that lay before us. As we ventured out into the lively London streets, I was thinking of the perils my feline friends were facing as we embarked upon the investigation.

"Right you are," Bill said, his voice steady and authoritative. "Let's not waste any more time. We have another victim to meet."

Westminster with its impressive buildings and rich history awaited us as we strode down the streets of Mayfair towards the River Thames.

"Ah, this must be it," Jessie remarked, gesturing to the luxury flat that stood before us. Its cream-coloured facade gleamed in the sunlight, a stark contrast to the dark waters of the Thames beside it.

"Ready for round two?" I quipped hoping to lighten the mood.

"Khan, you know there's nothing I enjoy more than unravelling the tangled threads of a mystery," Jessie said with a grin, her eyes alight with excitement. "Especially when cats are involved."

"Let's just hope our next victim is as forthcoming as Lady Street-Walters was," George said as he furrowed his brow no doubt contemplating the potential challenges ahead.

"That is quite the mouthful," I said.

"What is, Khan?" Jessie said.

"Lady Street-Walters," I said and with a grin, I added "SW from now on but not to her face."

"Incorrigible cat!" Jessie said and I simply grinned like my Cheshire counterpart.

"Only one way to find out if she is as forthcoming," Bill said getting us back on track, his tone firm yet reassuring. "Let's talk to her."

As we stepped into the luxury building, Jessie whispered, "Remember," as her eyes fixed on the flat door before us as she raised her hand to knock, "We're not just doing this for Lady Worthington and Fluffy or indeed, Lady Evelyn's friend, SW as Khan would say and her Mr Whiskers. We're doing it for all the victims – human and feline alike."

"Hear, hear," George said with a nod.

"Agreed," said Bill, "Let's see what our next interview holds."

The luxurious flat was bathed in the golden glow of the setting sun, casting long shadows across the opulent furnishings and polished floors. The River Thames flowed gracefully outside the large windows, the dark waters deceptive in that they were shimmering and glinting like liquid silver. Owing to my invisibility, I took my time to appreciate the view before turning my attention to the distraught woman seated on an elegant chaise longue.

"Mrs Langford," Jessie began gently, her hazel eyes radiating empathy. "We understand this must be an incredibly difficult time for you, and we can assure you that we are here to help. Can you please tell us what happened when you discovered your cat, Duchess, was missing?"

"Of course," Mrs Langford replied, her voice trembling as she dabbed at the corners of her tear-streaked eyes with a lace handkerchief. "I had just returned home from an afternoon of shopping at Harrods when I noticed that the door to Duchess's room was ajar. Upon entering, I saw that her bed was empty, and there was a ransom note demanding one thousand pounds for her safe return."

"Did you notice anything out of the ordinary leading up to her disappearance?" George asked, his brow furrowed as he leaned heavily on his cane while listening intently.

"Nothing at all," Mrs Langford sighed, her frustration evident. "Everything seemed so normal, and then suddenly, she was gone. I fear for her safety every moment she is away from me."

"Understandably so," Bill said. "Rest assured that we will do everything in our power to bring Duchess back to you. Now, have you had any contact with the kidnappers since receiving the ransom note?"

"None whatsoever," Mrs Langford replied, her eyes welling up with fresh tears. "I've been waiting by the telephone, praying for their call, but it hasn't come. I just... I need her back. She's more than just a pet; she's family."

"Of course, Mrs Langford," Jessie said softly, giving the woman's hand a reassuring squeeze. "We understand completely and will do everything we can to reunite you with Duchess."

"Thank you," she whispered, her voice cracking under the strain.

As we left the flat, the gravity of our task began to sink in. We had distraught victims and countless questions that needed answers. But as we stepped out into the cool London night, the city lights reflecting off the dark waters of the Thames, there was one thing that remained certain: we would not rest until justice was served and every beloved feline was returned to its rightful owner.

The London night air was still, damp and chilly, the perfect atmosphere for contemplation. I perched on Jessie's shoulder, my black fur juxtaposed against her auburn hair. We stood outside Mrs Langford's flat alongside George and Bill. The Thames whispered secrets in the background, its waters reflecting the moonlight as it brushed against the riverbanks.

"Alright," Jessie said, breaking the silence. "There can be no doubt there's a pattern here. All the victims received nearly identical ransom notes asking for the same sum of money."

"Indeed," George agreed, his breath visible in the cold air. "And all the kidnappings occurred within days of each other. This must be the work of an organized gang."

"An entire catnapping ring," I added. "How absolutely dreadful. And they're targeting wealthy pet owners, no less... and my clueless purebred feline friends."

"Exactly," Bill said, "we need to act swiftly if we want to solve this case and bring the culprits to justice. Time is not on our side, especially with the safety of these poor creatures hanging in the balance."

"I agree," Jessie said, "We should speak to all the victims and gather more information about their ransom demands and any potential leads. I think we need to do it because I am getting a feeling DI Ward is keeping us in the dark."

"Let's split up," George suggested, tapping his cane on the pavement. "Jessie, you and Khan can visit one victim while Bill and I visit another. We'll cover more ground that way and make faster progress."

"Reunited as a team," I said swishing my tail in agreement. "But let's not forget to keep our lines of communication open. We need to share any new findings promptly."

"Of course, Khan," Jessie said with a hint of a smile playing on her lips. "We wouldn't want to miss out on any of your valuable insights."

"Flattery will get you everywhere, my dear Jessie," I said allowing myself a small moment of levity before returning to the gravity of our task.

Chapter Four

SCOTLAND YARD

"Ah, Jessie, George and Bill, we have much to discuss," I said, my voice calm and measured as I leapt onto the Scotland Yard office's cluttered desk. My sleek black fur shimmered in the bright overhead light and my piercing green eyes were fixed on the three investigators who stood before me. They appeared astonished that I was taking the initiative.

"Your astonishment is understandable," I said with a hint of sarcasm lacing my words. "However, let us not waste time on trivial matters. We are here to solve the mystery of the kidnapped pedigree cats, are we not?"

"Of course," Jessie agreed, her eyes still full of surprise. "What do you propose, Khan?"

"First and foremost," I said, my tail flicking behind me as I paced across the desk, "we must gather intelligence from the feline community in London. They may hold crucial information that has eluded your human approach thus far. Ergo, yours truly will go undercover."

The three of them exchanged glances. I could almost hear the gears of their sharp minds turning as they considered my proposal. In the past, they had come to rely on my unique abilities and insights only a talking magical cat could provide. Still, they couldn't help but be wary of the potential risks involved.

"Alright," Jessie finally said. "We'll trust in your abilities once more, Khan. But first, we need to know how you plan on staying safe during this undercover mission."

"Rest assured, my dear Jessie," I replied with a hint of a smile, "I am more than capable of taking care of myself."

As I sat perched on the edge of the cluttered desk, I scrutinized the faces of Jessie, George, and Bill. I decided it was time to address the matter at hand. "I believe my unique abilities could be invaluable in solving this case," I said, my tone calm yet confident. The room fell silent as they processed my words.

Jessie's hazel eyes narrowed with curiosity and she stepped forward, her posture poised and attentive. "What exactly are you proposing, Khan?" she asked, her voice steady but laced with intrigue.

"Given the nature of this particular mystery," I began, curling my tail around me, "I think it only fitting that a cat should play a crucial role in unravelling its secrets."

"Are you seriously suggesting that you go undercover?" George inquired, his brow furrowed in scepticism but also concern for my well-being.

"Indeed," I replied, my emerald eyes meeting his. "I may be able to uncover information that would otherwise remain hidden from you." My whiskers twitched with amusement as I added, "After all, humans can be quite oblivious to the world of felines."

Jessie, always one to appreciate my wit, chuckled softly under her breath. She then turned to me, her expression serious once more. "And why help us, Khan? What's your thoughts when this mission could be dangerous?"

"Ah," I said, my lips curling into a faint smile, "first of all loyalty, dear Jessie. Loyalty to you and a desire to see justice served for the kidnapped cats." There was warmth in my voice, a testament to the bond we had forged over our many adventures together. "Secondly, like you, Bill, I don't like Ward's plan that we all go undercover. It is fraught with danger and I believe he knows that too."

Jessie nodded, her eyes shimmering with gratitude and understanding. "Very well," she agreed, extending a hand to rest gently on my sleek, black fur. "We'll trust in your abilities, Khan. Just be careful out there."

"Of course," I replied, my tail flicking in appreciation. "I shall return with the information we need to solve this perplexing mystery." And with that, I leapt gracefully from the desk, ready to embark on yet another clandestine mission in the shadows of London's feline underworld.

I paused because I saw George sceptically eyeing me. He seemed worried as he leaned on his cane. "Khan," he said, his tone cautious, "while Jessie seems to have faith in your abilities, I must admit that I'm still a bit... dubious. Perhaps you could provide some proof?"

"Proof of what?" I said.

"Your magic."

"George, that surprises me after all we have been through," I said, adding, "very well," I replied, unfazed by his request. My tail swished lazily as I focused my attention on a small paperweight on the desk. With a flick of my ear and a subtle shift of my gaze, the object began to rise slowly into the air, suspended by an unseen force.

George's eyes widened and for a moment, he was rendered speechless. "Well," he finally managed, clearing his throat, "I suppose that's sufficient evidence."

"Thank you, George," I said, lowering the paperweight back onto the desk with a soft thud. "Now, as for my plan, it involves going undercover within London's feline community. I will gather information about the kidnappings and report back to all three of you at the lodging house. That keeps DI Ward in the dark."

Jessie nodded but sounded concerned. "That sounds dangerous, Khan. Are you sure you're up for something like that?"

"Indeed," I confirmed, my whiskers twitching with determination. "The risks are worth taking if it means we can solve this case and bring justice to those responsible." I paced thoughtfully across the desk, the pads of my paws silent against the polished wood. "However, I must emphasize the importance of my role in this investigation. The cat underworld is not a place for the faint of heart."

A subtle grin spread across my whiskers as I observed Jessie and George exchange a glance, their determination to solve the case evident in their furrowed brows. These humans were truly fascinating creatures, always surprising me with their resilience and adaptability.

"Alright, Khan," Jessie said, her tone decisive. "We trust you and your abilities. Let's figure out how to make this undercover operation a success."

"Indeed," George added, stroking his moustache thoughtfully. "We must ensure your safety while you gather information within the feline community."

"First and foremost," I said, my tail flicking with authority, "I repeat we must keep Inspector Ward in the dark about our little plan. His involvement would only complicate matters."

"Agreed," George replied, nodding solemnly. "What else do we need to consider before you embark on this mission?"

"Communication will be key," I explained, pacing back and forth atop the desk. "I'll need a discreet way to relay any pertinent information I come across without arousing suspicion."

"Perhaps we could establish a meeting point?" Jessie suggested, her eyes alight with excitement. "Somewhere you can leave messages for us to find?"

"An excellent idea, Jessie," I praised, my ears perking up at her ingenuity. "A discreet location known only to the four of us. This should allow me to share my findings without jeopardizing the investigation. I still say the lodging house is the best bet because Mrs Swarbrick believes I'm your pet, Jessie. What about putting out a saucer of milk for me in the early mornings?"

"Splendid, Khan, you can update me with developments every morning, But in am emergency you can get a message to me telepathically, yes?" Jessie beamed.

"Of course, dear Jessie," Khan purred.

"Right," George said, "and what about your safety, Khan? How can we ensure you won't be discovered?"

"Ah, dear George," I purred, my green eyes twinkling with mischief. "That is where my unique talents come into play. Rest assured, I have more than a few tricks up my proverbial sleeve to evade detection."

"Very well," Jessie said. "But promise us you'll be careful, Khan. You're an invaluable member of this team, and we can't afford to lose you."

"Thank you for your kind words, Jessie," I acknowledged, my heart swelling with gratitude for their trust in me. "I assure you, I will do everything in my power to gather the necessary information and bring it back to you. But remember, patience is essential. Trust in my abilities, and together, we shall unravel this mystery."

With that, I leapt gracefully from the desk, my sleek black fur shimmering beneath the office's bright lighting. The stage was set, and our plans were laid out before us. It was time to delve into London's feline underworld and uncover the truth behind the kidnapped pedigree cats.

"Take care, Khan," George called after me, his voice tinged with both excitement and apprehension.

"Good luck," Jessie added, her gaze filled with a mix of admiration and concern.

The lamplight cast a bright glow in the office as I prepared to leave, my green eyes meeting Jessie's concerned gaze. "Fear not," I reassured her, my voice steady and comforting. "I shall keep you updated on my progress through telepathy. Your mind will be the first to know of any discoveries I make."

"Telepathy?" George raised an eyebrow, his eyes betraying his surprise. "Before today, that's a talent I didn't know you possessed, Khan."

"Ah, dear George," I replied, my whiskers twitching with amusement. "There is much about me that remains shrouded in mystery." My tail flicked thoughtfully as I continued, "but rest assured, my connection with Jessie will remain strong even amidst the chaos of London's feline underworld."

"Take care of yourself, Khan," Jessie implored, her freckled face etched with worry. "We're counting on you, but your safety is paramount."

"Thank you, Jessie," I said softly, touched by her concern. "Your confidence in me means more than you can imagine."

"Remember," George said leaning heavily on his cane, "if things become too dangerous, don't hesitate to retreat. We'll find another way."

"Your concern is noted and appreciated," I replied, nodding my head in acknowledgement. "But trust in my abilities and have faith that I will accomplish what I've set out to do."

Jessie smiled at me, her eyes brimming with admiration. "We believe in you, Khan. You've never let us down before."

"Indeed," Bill agreed, a hint of pride evident in his voice. "You truly are the enigmatic feline, aren't you?"

"Enigmatic indeed," I said giving them a wink. "But always loyal to my friends." With that, I turned and gracefully leapt onto the windowsill, surveying the bustling streets of London below.

"Good luck, Khan," Jessie whispered, her voice filled with hope and affection.

"Until we meet again," George added, his tone equal parts concern and anticipation.

"Until we meet again, my dear friends," I whispered before disappearing into the shadows ready to embark on my daring undercover mission. I nodded my head once more, my sleek black fur glistening in the lamplight. With a flick of my tail, I vanished into the night ready to embark on my daring undercover mission. The fate of the kidnapped pedigree cats rested in my paws, and I vowed not to let them down.

The moment Khan vanished into the shadows of London's streets, Jessie and George found themselves alone in the Scotland Yard office. They exchanged a glance filled with excitement and apprehension, the silence between them heavy with unspoken thoughts.

"Right," Jessie said breaking the silence as she straightened her shoulders. "We've got work to do ourselves. Khan may have his magical abilities, but we've got our own skills to put to use."

"I agree," George said, his eyes sparkling with determination. He steadied himself with his cane taking a deep breath to steady his nerves. "We mustn't waste any time. Let's go over our leads again, shall we?"

Jessie nodded and retrieved a notepad from her desk quickly flipping to a page filled with scribbled notes. She tapped a finger on the paper, her eyes flitting over the words as if they held the key to the mystery.

"According to our sources," she began, "the most recent cat to be kidnapped belonged to Lady Eleanor Fitzwilliam. It seems she was hosting a party at her home when the incident occurred."

"Perhaps someone attending the party knows something," George mused, stroking his fashionable moustache. "Though it would be prudent to check all guests thoroughly before questioning them."

"Agreed," Jessie concurred. "It's clear that the perpetrator is familiar with the upper-class circles these pedigree cats come from. We should start by interviewing Lady Eleanor's staff as well. Maybe one of them saw something."

"Excellent point," George replied. "I'll contact Inspector Ward and see if he can arrange for us to speak with the staff tomorrow morning. In the meantime, we should review the evidence we've collected so far and search for any possible connections between the victims."

As they delved deeper into their investigation, Jessie, George and Bill thought of their feline friend. They had seen Khan's magical powers in action before, but each time he ventured into danger, they couldn't help but worry for his safety.

"Khan will be fine," Jessie reassured George as if reading his thoughts. "He's far more resourceful than any ordinary cat."

"Indeed, and he is no ordinary cat, "Bill said, a small smile tugging at the corners of his lips. "I suppose we should have faith in our mysterious companion."

The three investigators gathered their notes, hats, and coats, preparing to venture out into the city once more. Their minds were filled with anticipation for Khan's return and the progress they hoped to make in solving the mystery of the kidnapped pedigree cats.

"Let's go, then," Jessie said. "We've got a case to solve and we can't let Khan down."

"Quite right," George replied, adjusting his homburg hat before leaving Scotland Yard and spilling out onto the bustling streets of London. "Onward, my dear Jessie, to unravel the secrets of the night."

Chapter Five

THE NEXT MORNING

Khan had not been in touch through telepathy or otherwise so Jessie left out a saucer of milk at the back door of the Vauxhall lodging house before she joined George and Bill for one of Mrs Swarbrick's ample English breakfasts. She only nibbled at her food though as she could not stop worrying about Khan. George guessed what was troubling her and checked himself to see if there was any sign of their beloved feline companion. Nothing. No sign of a cat and no milk having been disturbed.

"Jessie, there's no use worrying. He can take care of himself. Let's do what we do best and investigate. Mark my words, Khan will show up when he's good and ready," George said on Jessie's return to the dining room.

"He's right..." Bill said but stopped on seeing Jessie hold up her hand. Several minutes passed with Jessie holding that pose then she started scribbling notes frantically.

"Jessie, what is it? You're scaring me," George said.

Jessie beamed from ear to ear and stopped writing then said, "He's fine. That was Khan using our telepathic line of communication. I have made notes of what he told me. It's what he gleaned from the alley cats last night."

"Thank goodness he's okay. What did he have to say?" George said.

Looking at her notes, Jessie repeated the essence of what Khan had learnt, "The feline community are saying that it's not just pedigree cats that are being kidnapped but there is also a supernatural aspect in what these catnappers are up to..."

Bill interrupted, "Such as what?"

"He's not sure. He said some of the cats were talking about mystical creatures but when he asked what that meant, one of the alley cats described a peacock."

"So, they could be exotic creatures not mystical," George said solemnly.

"Perhaps," Jessie said, "but the peacock has a revered place in Greek and Chinese mythology. Khan also gave me some names of wealthy individuals who the cat fraternity say could be involved in the supernatural whether mystical or exotic creatures and some of them have died because they asked too many questions."

Bill took one look at Jessie's serious face and cottoned on, "Aye, lass, if Khan is passing this on then it must be investigated. Is that the list of names you have in front of you?"

"It is," she said.

"We have work to do. A certain Mr Radcliffe is the first on the list but we need to get a move on as Ward is looking for us and can't understand why we aren't undercover on his manor. Eventually, he will twig that we are doing our own thing," Bill said.

"I don't care about Ward. It's Khan who matters and I'm delighted we know he is well but you are right. Investigating is what we need to do," Jessie said. "One of these socialites on this list may hold the key to the mystery so remember," Jessie paused "... we need to build rapport and trust with these people. It's going to be essential if we want to get any information from the likes of them."

"Agreed." Bill said, his blue eyes focused on Jessie. "We have to tread carefully with most potential witnesses but especially with those wealthy folks. They're not always keen on sharing their secrets."

"Right," George said thoughtfully, tapping his cane against the floor. "We need to strike a balance between being assertive and empathetic."

With their strategy set, the trio ventured out into the crisp London air, making their way towards Southwark and the grand Georgian house of the first person on the list. As they approached the ornate wrought-iron gate, a formidable-looking butler appeared, eyeing them warily.

"Can I help you?" he asked, his tone guarded.

"Good morning, sir," Jessie replied with her most charming smile. "We're here to speak with Mr Radcliffe regarding a recent... incident involving one of his acquaintances. It's a delicate matter, but rest assured, our intentions are purely professional."

The butler hesitated, clearly suspicious, before reluctantly allowing them inside. Jessie quietly congratulated herself on her resourcefulness, knowing that gaining entry was only the first hurdle.

As they were led into an opulent drawing-room, they found Mr Radcliffe perched on a velvet armchair, his silver-handled cane resting against its side. He regarded them with a mixture of curiosity and suspicion, a single eyebrow raised in query.

"Mr Radcliffe," Jessie said, her tone respectful yet assertive, "we've come to seek your help in an ongoing investigation. We understand that you were acquainted with the late Lord Harrington and may have valuable information for us."

"Indeed?" Mr Radcliffe replied, clearly unimpressed. "And what makes you think I would be inclined to share such information with strangers?"

"Because," Jessie said, her voice softening, "we share a common goal: justice for those who can no longer speak for themselves. We know this is a difficult time for you and Lord Harrington's other friends, but any assistance you can provide could be crucial in solving this mystery."

The room fell silent as Mr Radcliffe considered her words, his eyes darting between Jessie, George, and Bill. Finally, he sighed and gestured for them to sit.

"Very well," he said. "I'll tell you what I know, but let's make this quick. I've little patience for prying investigators, no matter how charming they may be."

"Thank you, Mr Radcliffe," Jessie replied. "Your cooperation is greatly appreciated."

As the trio settled into their seats, Jessie knew that they had only just begun to chip away at the wealthy witnesses' resistance. But with her resourcefulness and unyielding pursuit of justice, she was confident that she could win over even the most reluctant witness.

As Mr Radcliffe began to share his story about Harrington and his dabbling in the trading of exotic creatures, George leaned back in his chair, one hand resting on his cane, the other cradling his pipe. His dark eyes shifted between their reluctant witness and the others in the room, observing every minute detail.

"Lord Harrington was quite a character," Radcliffe said, sipping his tea. "We were friends for many years, but there were times when I questioned his judgment."

"Indeed?" George said, a hint of dry amusement in his voice. "I've always found that people's judgments improve considerably when they're not around to make them."

Jessie suppressed a smile as she glanced at George who gave her a subtle nod. He had picked up on the same inconsistencies she had, and his dry wit seemed to have the intended effect: Mr Radcliffe chuckled and appeared more at ease.

"True enough, Mr Jenkins," he agreed, his guard lowering slightly. "But I digress. Lord Harrington had a penchant for collecting... shall we say... unusual artefacts. Some of which he believed held paranormal powers."

"Interesting," Bill Roberts said, his authoritative tone drawing focus. "And did you ever witness any evidence of these supposed powers?"

Mr Radcliffe hesitated, clearly uneasy with the direction of the conversation. Sensing this, Bill softened his approach. "I understand this may be difficult for you, sir. But rest assured, our aim is solely to uncover the truth and bring justice to those affected by any wrongdoings."

The empathy and professionalism in Bill's voice seemed to do the trick. Mr Radcliffe sighed, nodding his head. "There was one incident... I can't say for certain what happened, but it was unlike anything I'd ever seen before."

"Please, share it with us," Jessie encouraged gently, her compassionate demeanour mirrored by George's attentive gaze and Bill's calm reassurance. Together, they had managed to put Radcliffe at ease and information began to flow more freely.

"Well, all I can say was it was all very strange. There I was in Harrington's home when several ruffians burst in demanding money from my friend."

"Do you know why?" Bill said.

"Something to do with llamas, that's what I gathered," Radcliffe said.

"Did he call the police?" Jessie said.

"No and that was strange too."

As they continued their questioning, George's probing mind worked in tandem with Jessie's resourcefulness and Bill's expertise. With each witness, they encountered suspicion and resistance, but through their persistence and adaptability, they slowly peeled back the layers of secrecy surrounding the lives of the people on Khan's list.

And so, the investigation moved forward, propelled by the combined talents of Jessie Harper, George Jenkins, and Bill Roberts. Each success bolstered their confidence, and the truth they sought inched closer within their grasp.

Under the watchful gaze of an ornate grandfather clock, Jessie Harper leaned forward in her chair and locked eyes with Mrs Winthrop, a wealthy and high-strung socialite whose late husband had been on the list. The tension in the room was as tight as a piano wire as Jessie posed her question with careful precision.

"Mrs Winthrop, is there anything you can tell us about your husband's involvement with the paranormal?" Jessie asked, her hazel eyes unblinking.

The woman nervously adjusted her pearl necklace, her lips pursed in indignation. "I don't see how that's relevant," she replied icily. "And who are you to pry into our affairs like this?"

Jessie remained unfazed by the woman's resistance. "We're here to uncover the truth, Mrs Winthrop. And we believe that understanding the deceased' interest in the paranormal may be key to solving an important case."

"Indeed," George added as his dark eyes studied the witness. "There's no need to be alarmed, madam. We only wish to gather as much information as possible to ensure justice is served."

"Justice? What do you know of justice?" Mrs Winthrop snapped, her haughty tone betraying her suspicion. "For all I know, you could be charlatans trying to exploit our grief!"

"Mrs Winthrop, I assure you," Bill interjected, his voice firm yet caring. He showed her his identification – a warrant card in the name of Detective Sergeant William Lloyd Roberts of the Liverpool City Police. "Our intentions are pure, and our reputations speak for themselves. We understand that this is a difficult time, but your cooperation is essential for our investigation."

"Very well," Mrs Winthrop conceded begrudgingly, her eyes narrowing. "But I warn you, I will not tolerate any disrespect or insinuations about my late husband."

"Of course," Jessie replied graciously. "Now, if you could please tell us about any unusual occurrences or incidents involving your husband and the paranormal..."

As Mrs Winthrop began to share her account which was almost identical to that of Mr Radcliffe, Jessie, George, and Bill exchanged knowing glances. Their determination to uncover information remained unwavering even in the face of uncooperative witnesses. And as the trio navigated the delicate social dynamics of their affluent subjects, they knew that persistence would be key to getting close to the truth about the people on Khan's list.

"Very well," Jessie said, her voice steady as she pressed on with her questions. "And can you think of anyone else other than those ruffians who might have had a motive to harm your husband or any others he was involved with?"

"Absolutely not!" Mrs Winthrop snapped, her eyes flashing with anger. "They were all respectable people, unfairly targeted by this... this monster!"

"Monster? To whom do you refer?" Jessie said.

"Him... that Reginald Dawes. My husband was fine until he met Dawes and got involved with ruffians from the criminal underworld," Mrs Winthrop said.

"Ma'am, I am sorry to be blunt but was this involvement with Dawes the reason for your husband taking his own life?" George said.

Mrs Winthrop sighed, defeated by persistent and direct questioning, "You may continue your investigation, but I warn you – if you tarnish my husband's name, I will make sure your agency never works in this town again. Let me make this clear - make no mention of how my dear Earnest passed away."

"Understood, Mrs Winthrop. We appreciate your co-operation," Bill said, his professionalism shining through. "Now, let us leave you in peace and bring this interview to a close."

THE SOUND OF AN ornate French mantle clock echoed through the high-ceilinged drawing room of the townhouse belonging to Mrs Davenport. The clock's steady ticking punctuating the tension that hung in the air. Jessie Harper stood before the fireplace, her eyes fixed on the ornate marble mantle adorned with delicate China figurines. She took a deep breath and turned to face Mrs Eleanor Davenport, whose husband had also been on Khan's list. David Davenport had also taken his own life.

"Mrs Davenport," Jessie began, her voice softening as she addressed the grieving widow. "I understand how difficult this must be for you, but we're here to find out the truth and bring justice to your husband and the other victims."

Eleanor Davenport, a slender woman dressed in black mourning attire, dabbed at her reddened eyes with a lace handkerchief. "I appreciate that, Miss Harper," she whispered, her voice thick with emotion. "But I don't know what more I can tell you. My husband was a good man – he didn't deserve this."

"None of them did," Jessie agreed, her heart aching for the woman before her. "That's why we're so determined to find answers. If there's anything – no matter how small – that you think might help us, please don't hesitate to share it."

A flicker of appreciation crossed Mrs Davenport's tear-streaked face and she nodded. "Well, there is one thing," she hesitated, glancing nervously at George and Bill, who stood nearby, listening intently. "It's probably nothing, but... my husband mentioned a few weeks ago that he'd bumped into an old acquaintance while he was in town. He seemed... uneasy about it."

"Can you recall the name of this acquaintance?" George asked, his keen eyes betraying his interest.

"Um, I believe it was... Reginald. Yes, Reginald Dawes," Mrs Davenport confirmed, wringing her hands together as if trying to squeeze out more information.

"Thank you, Mrs Davenport," Jessie said warmly, sensing the woman's reluctance to share more. "You've been very helpful. We'll look into this Reginald Dawes and see if there's any connection."

As they left the Davenport residence, Bill said, "Reginald Dawes, eh? It might be worth looking into his background – see if there's anything that connects him to the others on the list."

"I agree, seeing he was known to Winthrop and Davenport who both took their own lives apparently a short time after making the acquaintance of our Mr Dawes," Jessie replied, her mind already buzzing with possibilities. "Who is next on the list?"

THE DETECTIVE TRIO APPROACHED the grand estate of their next person on Khan's list – a well-known industrialist named Edward Kingsley. As they stepped onto the manicured lawn, Jessie took note of the immaculate gardens and the imposing façade of the mansion. This was a man used to wielding power, and she knew she'd have to adapt her approach accordingly.

"Ah, there you are!" Kingsley appeared in the doorway, his booming voice carrying across the grounds. "I've been expecting you!" He ushered them inside, and Jessie couldn't help but be impressed by how forthcoming he seemed compared to Mrs Davenport. Bill wondered if he knew Dawes and if he did, why was he alive unlike Winthrop and Davenport.

"Thank you for agreeing to speak with us, Mr Kingsley," Jessie said as they settled into the lavish sitting room. She noticed him sizing her up and decided to rely on her resourcefulness to navigate the delicate social dynamics at play.

"Of course! Anything to help with your investigation," Kingsley replied, pouring himself a glass of brandy. "Now, what can I help you with?"

"Actually, we were hoping you might be able to shed some light on a gentleman named Reginald Dawes," George said.

"Reginald?" Kingsley raised an eyebrow. "Well, I suppose I might know a thing or two about him."

"Did you happen to notice any unusual behaviour from Mr Dawes before the incidents occurred? I am referring to the sad demise of Messrs Winthrop and Davenport," George asked, his sharp eyes studying Kingsley's reactions.

"Unusual? No, not really," Kingsley responded, a flicker of hesitation crossing his face. "He's always been a bit of a recluse, if you ask me."

George picked up on the subtle cue and pressed further. "Did you ever see him interact with either Mr Winthrop or Mr Davenport?"

Kingsley hesitated for a moment before answering. "Now that you mention it, I did see him in a huddle with those two gentlemen at a party a few weeks back. Seemed rather intense but I didn't think much of it at the time."

"Interesting," Jessie mused, filing away the information for later. "How would you describe their relationship?"

"Can't say for certain," Kingsley admitted, sipping his brandy. "But it was clear they were more than mere acquaintances."

"Thank you, Mr Kingsley," Jessie said, "We appreciate your candour and cooperation."

"Happy to help," Kingsley replied, a genuine smile crossing his face. "If there's anything else you need, don't hesitate to ask."

As they took their leave, Jessie couldn't shake the feeling that they'd possibly uncovered a crucial piece of the puzzle.

THE TRIO MADE THEIR way to the home of the next on the list that Khan had supplied. It was in the same area as the Kingsley residence.

As they entered the drawing room, Bill took the lead, his authoritative presence commanding attention. "Good evening, Mr and Mrs Wilkinson," he greeted warmly. "I'm

Detective Sergeant Roberts, and these are my associates, Miss Harper and Mr Jenkins. We appreciate your willingness to speak with us."

"Of course," replied Mrs Wilkinson, her eyes flicking between the three of them. "We'll do whatever we can to help."

"Thank you," Bill said, his empathetic nature shining through. "We understand this must be a difficult time for you."

"Indeed," Mr Wilkinson murmured, his face strained with worry.

Jessie took a deep breath and began the questioning under the watchful and experienced eye of Bill Roberts. As Jessie and the Wilkinsons spoke, Bill observed Jessie and George, tactfully providing quiet guidance and support when needed by instigating a fresh line of questioning. In this way, he shared his insights on investigative techniques, helping them navigate the delicate dance of gathering information from the wealthy couple.

"Mrs Wilkinson," George said thoughtfully, "you mentioned that your late friend, Lady Tremaine, had been acting strangely before her untimely death. Can you recall any specific incidents or encounters she may have had?"

"Let me think," Mrs Wilkinson said, her brow furrowing in concentration. Bill nodded approvingly, impressed by George's ability to pose questions that encouraged deeper thought.

"Actually," she continued, "there was one odd occurrence. A few days before her passing, I saw her speaking with a man I didn't recognize. She appeared quite agitated and hurried away as soon as their conversation ended."

"Interesting," Jessie said exchanging a glance with George. "Firstly, can you confirm Lady Tremaine took her own life? And did Lady Tremaine tell you the name of this man?"

"Yes, she took an overdose but they don't know if her death was accidental or suicide. As for the name… yes, but I have a terrible memory. I think the name started with the letter 'D.' Dawson… Dyer… No, that's not right but for some reason I want to say Dogs," Mrs Wilkinson said.

"Don't worry. It might pop into your head unexpectedly," Jessie said seeing Mrs Wilkinson was flustered.

"Do you remember anything about the man's appearance or demeanour?" Jessie said.

"Only that he seemed out of place," Mrs Wilkinson replied hesitantly. "A bit unkempt, and his clothing was rather shabby for our social circle."

"Anything else? Please take your time…" George said.

"Only that he appeared to be with another man who was better dressed and for some reason I can't shake the notion he was a detective."

"Thank you, Mrs Wilkinson," Bill interjected, his professionalism and empathy evident. "Your cooperation will help us immensely."

"Happy to assist," Mr Wilkinson added, offering them a supportive smile.

As they left the Wilkinson residence, it was clear they had made a small but significant breakthrough. The trio felt a growing confidence in their progress, knowing that every detail brought them closer to unravelling the mystery. With each witness they questioned, Jessie, George, and Bill Roberts believed they were closer to the truth.

With the Wilkinson interview behind them, Jessie, George, and Bill Roberts set off towards their next destination. The trio walked down the leafy streets of London their footsteps echoing in the crisp autumn air. As they turned a corner, they noticed a sleek black cat sauntering towards them. Khan's piercing green eyes locked onto Jessie as he approached, his regal bearing impossible to ignore.

"Ah, Khan," Jessie greeted him warmly. "I see you've been keeping an eye on things."

"Indeed," Khan replied. "I wouldn't want you humans to miss any important details."

"Much appreciated," George said, grinning at the cat's sarcasm. "Your feline instincts might prove invaluable."

"Speaking of instincts," Bill interjected, "I have a feeling our next witness might not be as cooperative as the Wilkinsons. We'll need all hands—or paws—on deck for this one."

"Agreed," Jessie nodded, "let's not waste any time, then."

As they approached the grand residence of the next person on the list, a sudden gust of wind sent a flurry of leaves dancing around their feet. Khan leapt gracefully into the air, batting at the swirling foliage with his paw. Jessie chuckled at the sight, momentarily lightening the tension that had been building within her.

"Always nice to see our feline friend enjoying himself," George commented, his dry wit bringing a smile to Jessie's face.

"Perhaps we should take a leaf out of his book," Jessie said, earning a chuckle from both men.

"Indeed," Bill agreed, his authoritative presence never faltering despite the momentary levity. "Now, let's prepare ourselves for this next interview."

The trio with Khan now invisible knocked on the imposing front door, which was soon opened by a stern-faced butler. They were led into a decadently furnished sitting room, where their next on the list awaited.

"Ah, Mr Montgomery," Bill began, using his direct manner to establish rapport. "Thank you for agreeing to speak with us."

The well-dressed man eyed them suspiciously, his haughty demeanour immediately putting Jessie on edge. She noticed Khan, invisible to all except her, George and Bill, slinking around the room, subtly making his presence known to his companions. His quiet confidence seemed to bolster her own resolve.

"Time is money," Mr Montgomery snapped, clearly unimpressed by their presence. "So, make it quick."

"Very well," Jessie said, her resourcefulness on full display as she dived into her line of questioning. "We understand that you were acquainted with the late Lady Tremaine. Did you notice anything unusual about her behaviour in the days leading up to her death?"

"Unusual?" Mr Montgomery scoffed. "I wouldn't say so. She was always a bit...flighty."

"Flighty?" George repeated, his analytical mind already searching for subtle cues and inconsistencies. "How so?"

"Let's just say she had a penchant for drama," Mr Montgomery replied evasively, earning a raised eyebrow from Jessie.

"Interesting," she said before pressing further. "And did any specific incidents come to your attention recently that might be relevant to our investigation?"

"Look," Mr Montgomery huffed, his patience wearing thin, "I've told you all I know. Now, if you'll excuse me, I have more important matters to attend to."

"Of course," Bill said smoothly, his empathy and professionalism shining through as he deftly navigated the delicate social dynamic. "We appreciate your time, Mr Montgomery."

As they left the residence, Jessie couldn't shake the feeling that they'd missed something crucial. But she knew they had no choice but to continue following the lead of the mysterious Mr Dawes and keep investigating to see if he had any part in the sad suicides.

"Khan, what do you make of it all? Did you find out any more from your feline friends on the street about Dawes and these seemingly connected deaths?" Jessie said.

"Not yet, Jessie, but give me more time," Khan said then disappeared in true mysterious fashion.

Chapter Six

Mrs Swarbrick was surprised and grateful at the same time when Jessie paid for another room at the Vauxhall lodging house. The team needed to use the room as a temporary office as they suspected there were prying eyes and ears at Scotland Yard and they weren't sure they could trust DI Ward so using an office at Clerkenwell Police Station was out of the question.

The team was in that office with George poring over a stack of notes on a small table in front of him. "Jessie, we can't keep going like this," George said rubbing his temple with one hand while gripping his cane with the other. "We need someone who can dig deeper into these old records and unearth hidden connections. Someone like Isabel."

"True. She is a very good receptionist but she's invaluable when it comes to research," Jessie said, leaning back in her creaky wooden chair as she gazed at the cluttered office, "her knowledge of obscure facts and ability to find patterns where others see chaos could be exactly what we need to crack this case wide open."

"Indeed. Remember that time she pieced together the connection between the smugglers and the haunted lighthouse? Saved us hours of chasing ghosts – both literally and figuratively." George chuckled at the memory, a grin crossing his face.

"Right," Jessie nodded, a slight smile tugging at the corner of her mouth. "So, let's bring her in on this one. I trust her abilities completely and I know she'll be a great addition to our team."

"Who will look after the Liverpool office if we bring Isabel down here?" George asked.

"Her sister, Agnes," Jessie said.

"Alright," George replied.

Two Days Later

Isabel arrived in London excited at the prospect of what she saw as a stepping stone to a promotion as she harboured ambitions to be another detective at the Dale Street Private Investigations Agency but she was unsure of herself. She wasted no time in researching aspects of the catnapping case.

"Jessie. George, I am so excited to get started researching the catnappings," Isabel exclaimed breathlessly clutching a stack of old newspapers under one arm as she rushed into the makeshift temporary office which now doubled as her room. Her eyes widened with curiosity as she took in their serious expressions. "What's going on?"

"We could ask you the same question," Jessie said nodding at the stack of newspapers under her arm.

Isabel hesitated for a moment, her gaze flitting between the two detectives before finally settling on the stack of newspapers in her hands. A determined gleam appeared in her eyes as she said, "Alright then, I'll start here."

Jessie and George assumed Isabel was referring to her research into the old newspaper archive now deposited on the desk in front of her but they knew she was a little eccentric so right now, it was all a guessing game.

Jessie to find out what Isabel was talking about said, "Are you referring to those old newspapers or something else?"

"I'm not sure. I'm nervous you see," Isabel said.

"I see," Jessie said, "can I ask you this and please be honest. Are you okay with working in the field as well as the research?"

Isabel's mismatched socks—one a vivid shade of pink, the other a bright yellow—peeked out from beneath her skirt as she crossed her legs and leaned back in her chair. Her wrists jangled with an assortment of colourful bracelets, drawing attention to her slender hands that were currently fidgeting with a pencil. The desk before her was cluttered with stacks of books, scattered papers, the newspaper archive, and half-empty cups of tea, creating a chaotic yet oddly endearing workspace.

"Jessie, George," she began, her brow furrowing with concern, "I appreciate your faith in my abilities, but I'm not sure if I'm cut out for field work. My strength has always been researching from the safety of an office or a library. I don't want to break any rules or get into trouble."

"Isabel," Jessie replied gently, "we wouldn't ask for your help if we didn't believe in you. We're not looking for you to be on the front lines. It's your research skills and unique insights that are invaluable to our investigation."

"Exactly," George chimed in, nodding his agreement. "We've seen how valuable your contributions have been in the past. You have nothing to worry about—we're in this together."

As Isabel chewed on her lip thoughtfully, she couldn't help but remember the times when her research had indeed made a difference in their cases. But still, the idea of getting involved in an investigation that might push her beyond her comfort zone was daunting even though she did have ambitions.

Isabel's fingers drummed against the edge of her cluttered desk, her mismatched socks tapping an uneven rhythm on the wooden floor. Her hesitation was slowly giving way to the thrill of adventure that danced in her veins. The challenge ahead was too tantalising to resist.

"Alright," she said hesitantly, looking up at Jessie and George, "I'm flattered. But what exactly do you expect me to do? I mean, besides my usual research?"

Jessie leaned forward, "You'll be our secret weapon, Isabel. Your knowledge of obscure information is unparalleled – occasionally we might need you in the field with us."

"Think about it," George said leaning on his cane, his dark eyes alight with determination. "Not only will you be putting your skills to the test, but you'll be experiencing firsthand the thrill of solving mysteries. It's not just about the research; it's about being part of something bigger."

Isabel considered their words, her thoughts racing. She had always been content working behind the scenes, poring over books and uncovering hidden connections. But now, the prospect of joining Jessie and George in their investigations stirred a newfound sense of purpose within her.

"Besides," Jessie continued, sensing Isabel's hesitation, "I think you've always wanted to step out from behind that desk and see what we really do. This is your chance, Isabel. Think of the personal growth and excitement waiting for you out there!"

Isabel's heart swelled with pride as she absorbed their words. The desire to prove herself, to be part of something greater than herself, was too powerful to ignore.

"Alright," she said, determination creeping into her voice. "I'll do it. I'll join you in the field."

"Brilliant!" Jessie exclaimed, clapping her hands together.

"Welcome aboard," George said, offering a warm smile.

Together with Jessie and George, they would face whatever mysteries awaited them – and she couldn't wait to get started.

"Wait," Isabel said, her enthusiasm momentarily stalled. She looked between Jessie and George, her brow furrowed with concern. "I don't want to put any of us in danger or jeopardise the agency's reputation. Can you promise me that we'll be safe?"

Jessie shared a glance with George, understanding the gravity of Isabel's question. It was true that their line of work came with risks, but they had always managed to navigate those dangers together.

"Isabel," Jessie began, as she held the gaze of the younger woman, "we can't make promises about what might happen during an investigation. But we can promise you this: George and I will always prioritise our safety and yours and we'll work as a team to overcome any challenges we may face."

George nodded as he added his own reassurance. "We've been through some difficult situations before, and we've come out of them stronger and wiser. You have our word that we'll do everything in our power to keep you safe."

Isabel hesitated for a moment, taking in their assurances. She knew they were sincere in their commitment to her safety, and she also realised that she had much to gain from this opportunity. Risk was inherent in any worthwhile pursuit, and if she truly wished to grow and test her abilities, she would need to confront her fears head-on.

"Alright," she said softly, offering Jessie and George a tentative smile. "I trust you both. "I'm ready to face whatever challenges come our way."

"Excellent," Jessie beamed, clapping her on the shoulder. "We'll all watch out for each other, just like we've always done."

Isabel's eyes sparkled and she straightened her back, a grin spreading across her face. "Alright then, let's do this!" She said drunk on a contagious enthusiasm.

Jessie and George exchanged proud smiles as they watched Isabel hurriedly hang up her mismatched coat and an eccentric hat adorned with feathers of various colours. The sight of her peculiar attire only added to the sense of adventure that now enveloped them all.

"Welcome aboard, Isabel. We're thrilled to have you on the team," George said warmly, extending his hand. As she shook it firmly, Jessie caught a glimpse of the colourful bracelets jingling on her wrist, each one a testament to her unique personality.

"Thank you," Isabel replied, still beaming. "I promise I'll give it my all."

As THE TRIO HUDDLED together ready to embark on the next phase of the catnapping investigation, I, Khan, silently watched from my perch on the windowsill. I was aware of the challenges that lay ahead but knew that my presence would provide an extra layer of protection for the team and I needed to reassure Isabel who had only known me as Jessie's pet cat.

With a sly grin, I couldn't help but add a touch of levity to the moment. "Well, it seems you've finally assembled a team worthy of my talents," I drawled, my green eyes shining with amusement. "Just try not to slow me down too much, will you?"

Jessie and George erupted in laughter at my remark, but it took some minutes for Isabel to realise she had heard a cat talk.

"You will get used to it and his other tricks like making himself invisible," Jessie said.

On cue, I became invisible leaving Isabel perplexed as she now saw nothing perched on the windowsill. Isabel shrugged and then smiled.

With spirits high, the newly expanded team were ready and eager to tackle the mysteries that awaited them. Little did they know, their journey together had only just begun.

Chapter Seven

THE AIR HUNG HEAVY with the scent of anticipation as I, Khan, prowled the streets of Clerkenwell. The moon cast a spectral glow over the cobblestones of the narrow alleyways and my sleek black fur seemed to absorb the shadows themselves rendering me all but invisible. As I crept through the narrow passages, my piercing green eyes probed the darkness for any sign of the hidden network of catnappers that Jessie, George, and Bill Roberts were so desperately trying to uncover.

"Ah, London," I thought, "a city of secrets, where every corner holds another mystery to solve—or create." My thoughts drifted briefly to my own mysterious past shrouded in ancient civilisations but I shook them off. There would be time for reminiscing later; tonight, I had a job to do.

As I rounded a corner, I caught sight of a group of suspicious individuals huddled together hiding in a doorway. They exchanged furtive glances and whispered words, their tension obvious even from a distance. My instincts told me they were up to no good and I couldn't help but feel a spark of excitement at the prospect of thwarting their plans. After all, what's life without a bit of drama? Come to think of it, what's life about without a bit of thwart. I stifled a chuckle at the thought of my brilliant humour.

"Time to see what these miscreants are up to," I thought, stealthily tuning in to their conversation from a safe distance. My paws made no sound on the damp cobblestones as I slunk closer, my senses heightened by the thrill of the hunt.

"Oi, you got the goods?" one of the men hissed casting a nervous glance over his shoulder. His voice was rough and gravelly like he'd swallowed a handful of pebbles.

"Keep your voice down!" his companion snapped. He was clutching a small cloth sack protectively to his chest. "Don't want anyone overhearing us now, do we?"

"Right, right," the first man muttered, his eyes darting around the alley. "So, we got what they want, yeah?"

"Of course," the man with the sack replied smugly. "Top-quality merchandise, just like always."

"Really? I can't help but wonder if you're simply trying to sell him a bag of rats," I thought, stifling a chuckle as I imagined their expressions if they knew they were being watched by a cat—a talking one, at that.

They moved away from the doorway so I continued to follow the group. My curiosity was piqued by their secretive behaviour. What were they hiding in that sack? Could it be connected to the catnappings? Or some other nefarious activity? As I trailed behind them, I sensed a feeling of satisfaction. Unbeknownst to these lowlifes, they were possibly leading me straight to the answers Jessie and George so desperately sought.

"Ah, the sweet taste of intrigue," I whispered to myself, my tail flicking with anticipation. "There's truly nothing quite like it."

The night air felt crisp and electric as I followed the suspicious individuals through the dimly lit passageways of Clerkenwell. They hadn't changed much since Dickensian times when they were full of scoundrels, rogues and vagabonds. My feline senses were on high alert, keenly attuned to every sound and movement. As we approached a seemingly abandoned warehouse, I felt a familiar thrill of excitement at the prospect of uncovering their secrets.

"Ah, this must be their lair," I thought, watching from the shadows as they entered the dilapidated building casting cautious glances over their shoulders. "How delightfully cliché."

I knew that my current form would be far too conspicuous for infiltrating the warehouse undetected. With a deep breath, I tapped into my ancient magical abilities and focused on the image of a small mouse. In an instant, my sleek black fur receded, and my body shrank down to the size of a mere rodent. The transformation was both swift and seamless – a testament to my mastery of the arcane arts.

"Goodbye, Enigmatic Feline," I whispered, my voice now a tiny squeak. "Hello, Mighty Mouse."

As a mouse, I scurried towards the warehouse, nimbly navigating through gaps in the crumbling brickwork. My new perspective made the world seem vast and imposing, yet I felt a surge of confidence knowing that I could slip past even the most watchful eye.

"Nobody suspects the humble mouse," I thought with a smirk, my whiskers twitching in amusement as I squeezed through a narrow crack in the wall.

Inside the warehouse, I paused for a moment to adjust to the darkness. My minuscule size may have granted me stealth, but it had also limited my vision. The faint light that streamed in through the grimy windows did little to illuminate the cavernous space.

"Ah well, guess I'll have to rely on my other senses," I mused, closing my beady eyes and focusing on the sounds echoing through the warehouse.

The hushed voices of the catnappers grew louder as I scurried closer, their whispered conversations revealing snippets of vital information. I listened intently, straining to catch every word while staying hidden in the shadows.

"Careful now, Khan," I reminded myself, my mouse heart pounding with a mixture of fear and exhilaration. "One false move, and you'll go from an Enigmatic Feline to a rodent's last stand."

As the adrenaline coursed through my tiny veins, I couldn't help but feel a profound sense of satisfaction at the thought of outwitting these criminals and helping Jessie and George in their quest for justice. My whiskers twitched with anticipation as I continued to gather intelligence knowing that each piece of the puzzle brought us one step closer to solving the mystery of the catnappings.

"Aha, the game is afoot!" I whispered to myself, a mouse-sized grin spreading across my face. "And may the best creature win."

The warehouse loomed around me like a sinister fortress and I could feel its oppressive atmosphere pressing down on my tiny mouse form. The scent of fear hung heavy in the air, mingling with the unmistakable aroma of feline distress. My whiskers quivered as I crept forward, each cautious step bringing me closer to the catnappers and their captives.

"Alright, Khan," I whispered to myself, steadying my nerves as I navigated the shadowy recesses of the warehouse. "It's showtime."

I inched my way toward the source of the voices, my heart pounding in tempo with each human vowel and consonant echoing through the vast space. As I rounded a corner, I caught sight of the catnappers – a motley crew if ever there was one – huddled around a table strewn with maps and ledgers, their expressions a mixture of greed and malice.

"Right, mates," said one of the men, his voice dripping with arrogance. "We've got our hands on some prime merchandise 'ere, and we can't afford any slip-ups." He gestured toward a cluster of cages containing the kidnapped pedigree cats, who cowered in fear, their once-proud coats now matted and filthy.

"Oi, be careful with that one!" snapped another catnapper, shoving his companion roughly as he manhandled a particularly frightened Siamese. "These are valuable animals, not your average alley cats."

"Enough bickering, you fools!" hissed a third man, his eyes narrowed into cold slits. "We need to focus on our next move. Our clients are growing impatient."

As I watched them from my hiding place, the catnappers continued to discuss their plans, and I noticed the callous disregard with which they treated the helpless cats. Anger surged through me, and I knew I had to do everything in my power to bring these villains to justice.

"Stay focused, Khan," I reminded myself as I listened intently to their conversation. "Every word counts."

"Let's go over the plan one more time," said one man who seemed to be the leader. He tapped a map with his greasy finger. "We'll move the cats tonight disguised as a shipment of textiles. Once they're safely delivered to our clients, we'll collect our payment and be out of here before anyone's the wiser."

"Sounds perfect," said another catnapper, rubbing his hands together eagerly. "No one will suspect a thing."

As I continued to gather crucial information about the catnappers' methods and connections, I couldn't help but feel a mix of excitement and dread. Jessie, George, and Bill Roberts needed to know what I'd uncovered – and fast.

"Alright, Khan," I thought as I prepared to make my escape, shifting my weight from one tiny paw to the other. "Time to put that feline agility to good use."

With one last glance at the cats who'd been ripped from their homes, I darted back through the shadows, vowing to myself that I would not rest until we had brought the catnappers to justice and reunited the stolen pets with their rightful owners.

"Justice will prevail," I whispered to myself as I slipped through the warehouse's cracks once more. "And this mouse-cum-cat has got their tails."

A gust of wind swept through the narrow alleyway, causing me to shudder as I shifted back from my mouse form into my true feline self. The transformation was always a bit unsettling but it was necessary if I wanted to relay the valuable information I had just gathered. My sleek black fur bristled in the chilly London air and I quickly darted across the cobblestone streets, eager to reunite with Jessie, George, and Bill Roberts, so I made my way to Vauxhall.

"Ah, there they are," I thought as I spotted Jessie, George, Bill and Isabel huddled together near a lamp-post outside the Vauxhall lodging house, their breaths visible in the cold night. Their faces were etched with concern and I couldn't help but feel a pang of pride knowing that I was about to ease their minds and provide the lead they so desperately needed.

"Evening, good humans," I greeted them confidently as I sauntered up to their feet, my signature wit evident in every word. "I trust you've been keeping warm while I've been gathering scintillating secrets."

"Khan!" Jessie exclaimed, relief washing over her face as she knelt to stroke my fur. "What did you find out?"

"Ah, where to begin?" I mused, pretending to ponder for dramatic effect. "Well, first off, it seems our catnappers are planning quite the feline heist tonight – moving their precious cargo under the guise of a textile shipment."

"Textiles?" George raised an eyebrow, his analytical mind already churning away at the implications. "Interesting choice."

"Indeed," I agreed before continuing. "They're quite pleased with themselves and confident that their plan will go off without a hitch. But we'll see about that, won't we?"

"Absolutely," Bill chimed in, his eyes steely with determination. "But we need more information, Khan. Were you able to find out anything about their connections or clients?"

"Ah, yes," I purred, my green eyes gleaming with satisfaction. "It seems that our feline felons have a rather extensive network of unsavoury characters aiding them in their nefarious deeds. And as for the clients... well, let's just say there's quite a market for pedigree cats among certain circles."

Jessie gritted her teeth, anger flashing in her hazel eyes. "We need to stop them, Khan. We can't let them get away with this."

"Of course, dear Jessie," I reassured her, rubbing my head against her leg affectionately. "That's why I'm here – to help you bring these miscreants to justice and reunite those poor cats with their loving families."

"Alright then," George said, straightening his posture and gripping his cane tightly. "We don't have much time. Let's go over the details and come up with a plan."

"Lead the way, my good man," I encouraged him, my tail flicking with anticipation. "I'm all ears – and whiskers."

As we prepared for action, I felt proud of my role within the team. Together, we would expose the catnappers and put an end to their cruel schemes.

I stretched my legs with a contented purr, watching as Jessie, George, Bill Roberts and Isabel absorbed the information I had relayed to them. Their faces conveyed a mix of shock, determination, and urgency – a powerful combination that would undoubtedly fuel their next course of action.

"Khan," Jessie began, "your intelligence is invaluable. We need to move quickly and investigate this warehouse before they have a chance to move the cats or cover their tracks."

"Agreed," George said, tapping his cane thoughtfully on the floor. "We'll need a plan to approach the warehouse without alerting them to our presence. Any suggestions?"

Bill rubbed his chin, his blue eyes looking to the clear sky as he considered their options. "We could split up and approach from different directions. That way, we can cover more ground and minimise the chances of being detected."

"An excellent idea, Detective Sergeant Roberts," I purred, my green eyes twinkling with mischief. "After all, as the saying goes, 'divide and conquer!'"

Jessie allowed herself a small smile at my comment, despite the seriousness of the situation. "Alright, let's get going. We don't have much time."

With a sense of urgency, the group set off towards the warehouse in Clerkenwell. As we walked, I couldn't help but notice the way Jessie and George exchanged subtle glances – a testament to the strong bond they shared not only as colleagues but also as something more.

The cobblestone streets echoed with human footsteps and the distant hum of activity from London's nightlife served as a stark contrast to the darkness that enveloped us. I stayed close to Jessie, my heightened senses on alert for any signs of danger or interference.

As we neared the warehouse, that shiver of excitement ran down my spine. I knew that with our formidable team, we stood a strong chance of exposing the catnappers and bringing them to justice.

"Remember," Jessie whispered as we paused to survey the area around the warehouse, "we need to be discreet and gather as much evidence as possible. If we play our cards right, we can put an end to this operation for good."

"Let's do this," George murmured. Bill partnered Isabel with Jessie, George and I taking our designated routes towards the warehouse so we had all the exits covered.

The moon cast an eerie glow over the dilapidated warehouse, its beams slicing through the mist that swirled around us. I could sense Jessie's heart pounding in her chest as we approached the entrance, her auburn hair pulled back into a bun to keep it out of her way.

"Can't say this place screams 'welcome,'" George muttered, his cane tapping rhythmically on the ground.

JUST A FEW HUNDRED yards away, Bill and Isabel were approaching one of the exits. "Let's hope the catnappers are taken by surprise," Bill Roberts said, his eyes checking the area for any signs of activity.

"Alright," Jessie whispered, taking a deep breath. "Bill and Isabel must be in place by now. We need to be quick and quiet. Remember, we're looking for anything that can help us uncover the truth behind this operation."

With a nod, we slipped inside the warehouse, human footsteps muffled by the thick layer of dust that coated the floor. The air was heavy with the scent of decay, and I couldn't help but shudder at the thought of the poor cats held captive here.

"Khan," Jessie murmured, glancing down at me as we stood in the gloomy interior, "you know what to do."

"Of course," I replied telepathically, my whiskers twitching with anticipation. "I'll cover the ground level and report back anything I find."

"Good luck, Khan," George said softly, giving me a reassuring pat before he and Jessie took up positions guarding the entrance we had just used to gain access to the warehouse.

As they disappeared, I focused my keen senses on the task at hand. My ears pricked up at the sound of distant scurrying – most likely mice seeking refuge from the cold night air. But there was something else, a faint vibration that set my fur on edge. I moved into telepathic mode.

"Jessie," I thought, "I think there might be something hidden beneath the floorboards."

"Really?" her hazel eyes widened in surprise. "How can you tell?"

"Call it a... feline intuition," I replied with a hint of amusement.

"Alright then, let's find a way down there."

Jessie and George joined me and we carefully made our way through the warehouse, "Over here," Jessie whispered, her hand resting on a concealed trapdoor. "I think this might lead to whatever is beneath the floorboards."

"Excellent work, my dear," I thought as she slowly lifted the door, revealing a set of rickety wooden stairs.

"Stay close, Khan," Jessie cautioned as the three of us descended into the darkness below.

"Wouldn't dream of being anywhere else," I said, my tail brushing against her leg as we navigated the narrow stairway.

The room beneath the warehouse was damp and musty, but there was no mistaking the faint sound of whimpering that echoed through the space.

"Jessie," I thought urgently, "we need to hurry. I can hear the cats – they're terrified."

"Right," she said, her voice trembling slightly. "Let's split up and see what we can find. But be careful, Khan – we don't know what else might be lurking down here."

"Understood," I assured her, my heart pounding with a mix of fear and determination as we ventured deeper into the hidden room, each searching for evidence that would help us unravel the mystery of the catnappers and bring them to justice.

The dim glow of a single flickering lightbulb cast eerie shadows on the cold, concrete floor as we cautiously stepped into the hidden room. My heart ached for the terrified felines imprisoned in the rows of cages that lined the walls; their pitiful cries reverberated through my bones and stirred a fierce protectiveness within me.

"Khan, this is ghastly," Jessie whispered, her voice trembling with a mix of disgust and determination. "We need to document everything and get these poor creatures out of here."

"Couldn't agree more," I replied, my eyes narrowing as I took in the deplorable conditions surrounding us. "Let's get to work."

As Jessie and George began examining the cages, Bill Roberts with Isabel kept watch at the entrance to the hidden room having made their way to join us from the other exit.

"Look at this," George murmured, pointing to a small emblem etched into one of the cages. "It appears to be some sort of crest. Could be useful in tracing the cats' origins."

"Well spotted, George," Jessie said, "make sure you get a photograph."

George had beaten Jessie to it. He had already fetched his compact Kodak with a built-in flash bulb from his satchel and snapped away.

"Let's keep looking for any other potential evidence." Jessie said.

I weaved my way between the cages using my mystical abilities to communicate with the frightened felines. The stories they shared with me were harrowing, each one ripped from the loving embrace of their families by nefarious hands. My resolve to bring these catnappers to justice only grew stronger with every heartbreaking tale.

"Khan, come look at this," Jessie called, beckoning me over to a cage containing a particularly regal-looking Siamese cat. "There's something different about this one."

"Allow me," I offered, extending a paw to gently touch the cat's quivering body. As I delved into her thoughts, an image of a grand estate materialized in my mind. "She belongs to a wealthy family – the crest on her collar matches that of their coat of arms."

"Excellent work, Khan," Jessie praised, her eyes shining with admiration and gratitude. "We'll make sure she's returned to her rightful home."

"Thank you, Khan," the Siamese cat whispered, her eyes conveying a depth of gratitude words could not express.

"Of course, my dear," I said softly, offering her a comforting nuzzle. "It's the least we can do for our fellow felines."

As we continued documenting the evidence, George's dry wit occasionally cut through the heavy atmosphere, bringing a much-needed touch of levity to the grim situation.

"Really, Jessie," he quipped as he snapped a photograph of a particularly ornate cage, "you should consider branching out into architectural photography. You've certainly got an eye for capturing the... less charming aspects of London's hidden spaces."

"Very funny, George," Jessie retorted, playfully swatting at his arm with a gloved hand. "But let's leave the jokes for later, shall we? We have work to do."

"Right you are, my dear," George conceded, his eyes crinkling with amusement as he returned to his task.

With our careful examination of the cages complete, we regrouped to discuss our findings and plan our next steps. "Alright, team," Jessie said, "we've gathered valuable information here. Let's get these cats to safety and bring these catnappers to justice."

"Agreed," I thought, my tail twitching with anticipation as we prepared to embark on the next leg of our mission. "Justice will be served – on a silver platter, no less."

As I perched atop a stack of crates, observing Jessie, George, and Bill Roberts completing their documentation of the hidden room, a feeling of unease settled in my sleek feline form. I couldn't help but think that there was something more to be discovered here.

"Wait," I meowed suddenly, drawing the attention of my human counterparts. "There's something we're missing. Something important." My whiskers twitched with certainty as I leapt down from the crates and began sniffing around the walls, tracing the air currents for any signs of hidden compartments.

"Khan's usually right," Jessie agreed, "we need to dig deeper."

"Alright then," George said, leaning on his cane as he joined us in our search. "Let's find what these ruffians are hiding."

"Ruffians?" Bill said with an amused smile. "Maybe you've been spending too much time with Khan, George. Next thing we know, you'll be chasing mice and scratching furniture."

"Ha! You'd like that, wouldn't you, Bill?" George shot back. "But I assure you, my affinity for cats hasn't extended quite that far."

Amidst the banter, my sensitive nose led me to a concealed panel near the floor. "Here!" I yowled triumphantly. "This wall isn't solid; there's something behind it!"

Jessie crouched down beside me, her fingers probing the seams of the panel. With a soft click, the hidden compartment swung open to reveal a dusty ledger filled with names, addresses, and other incriminating information no doubt about the catnappers and their clients.

"By Jove, Khan, you've done it again!" George exclaimed, his face alight with excitement.

"Indeed," Jessie added, her voice laced with determination. "This could be the key to bringing these criminals down."

"Let's get this photographed and collect any other evidence we can find," Bill suggested, his gruff voice betraying a hint of admiration for our feline companion.

As Geoge got to work with his camera snapping pictures of the ledger and searching for other evidence, I couldn't help but feel a swell of pride. My instincts had been correct and now we were one step closer to solving this mystery.

"Khan," Jessie said softly as she knelt beside me, a warm smile on her lips, "you're truly an invaluable member of this team."

"Thank you, Jessie," I purred, my heart swelling with affection for my human friends. "Now let's put these catnappers behind bars where they belong."

"Absolutely," agreed George, "that is the only disappointment that they weren't here when we raided the place." He snapped the last photograph before carefully closing the hidden compartment.

The dim light filtering through the warehouse's grimy windows cast eerie shadows on the walls as we carefully made our way towards the exit, each of us clutching a piece of crucial evidence. Jessie and George exchanged hushed whispers, their voices barely audible over the creaking floorboards and the distant hum of traffic outside.

"Can you believe what we found?" Jessie asked, her eyes wide with disbelief.

"Hardly," George admitted, his grip tightening on the cane he used for support. "This ledger could change everything."

"Indeed," I added, my feline senses picking up on their excitement. "It's not every day one stumbles upon such a treasure trove of information."

As we neared the warehouse door, the magnitude of our find still loomed large in my mind. The names and addresses in that ledger would undoubtedly lead us to the heart of the catnapping operation, and perhaps even to its nefarious mastermind. My whiskers twitched in anticipation. This was the breakthrough we had been waiting for, and now, justice was within our reach.

"Khan," Jessie said, looking down at me with a mixture of gratitude and affection, "we couldn't have done this without you."

"Of course not," I replied with a wry grin. "You humans may be clever, but sometimes it takes a cat's keen instincts to sniff out the truth."

George chuckled softly, his dark eyes alight with amusement. "Well, we certainly wouldn't be standing here without your help, Khan. Your contributions to this case have been invaluable."

"Thank you, George," I purred, feeling a warm glow inside of me. "Now let's get out of here and put this new-found knowledge to good use."

With a nod, Jessie cautiously pushed open the warehouse door, revealing the moonlit streets of Clerkenwell beyond. As we stepped outside, a cool breeze ruffled my fur, and I couldn't help but shiver at the thought of what lay ahead. The path to justice was fraught with danger and this caper is not finished yet.

"Alright, team," Jessie said, her tone firm and determined, "let's head back to Vauxhall and put together a plan to bring these catnappers down."

"No, Jessie, first we must contact Lady Pandora Street-Walters who will telephone the Commissioner so the cats will be rescued," George said.

"Yes, of course," Jessie said,

Bill seemed to be growing impatient. His jaw set and eyes narrowing as he surveyed the desolate streets before he spoke. "We've got work to do. But I do think Khan and George should stay here until the cats are safe."

"Good idea, that makes sense," George said.

As Jessie, Isabel and Bill left the warehouse behind and ventured into the night, I felt a curious blend of excitement and trepidation coursing through me. We were one step closer to unravelling this mystery and bringing the villains to justice but I knew that our journey was far from over. Yet, with my loyal human companions at my side, I was certain that no obstacle would prove insurmountable.

"Come on, Khan," Bill called, beckoning me to his side. "We've got to keep look out."

With a flick of my tail, I bounded up to him prepared to wait until the cats were safe then later to confront the challenges that awaited us and to restore peace to the feline residents of London.

THE COMMISSIONER OF THE Metropolitan Police was miffed at receiving a phone call late at night but as it was Lady Street-Walters who was calling, he immediately arranged for a fleet of vans to go to the warehouse and rescue the cats.

Bill and I watched with pride as the prize pedigree cats were transferred to the police vans and taken to safety. Bill was the only human who understood who the rescued cats were waving to because I had adopted my cloak of invisibility.

Chapter Eight

THE NEXT MORNING

The grand edifice of New Scotland Yard built in a distinctive banded red brick and white Portland stone, loomed before us as our taxi pulled to the curb. I hopped out, my feline grace on full display. Jessie paid the driver while George gathered their bags. Isabel followed clutching a briefcase.

"Another day, another catnapping case to solve," I quipped, stretching languidly on the sidewalk. "The glamorous life of a paranormal detective, eh?"

Jessie shot me a wry smile. "Come on, Khan. Let's not keep Bill waiting."

We strode into the bustling lobby, the heels of my human colleagues clicking smartly on the polished floor. I padded alongside them, my fur gleaming under the electric lights but I was invisible to all except for the team. Bobbies and plainclothes detectives hurried to and fro barely sparing a glance for the unlikely trio in their midst -

a sharp-eyed woman, another woman with mismatching stockings and a dapper gent holding a cane.

Detective Sergeant Bill Roberts greeted us at the lift, his reddish hair neatly combed and his blue eyes bright with anticipation. "Jessie, George, Isabel, good to see you. And Khan, always a pleasure." He gave me a respectful nod, which I returned with a flick of my tail.

"What have you got for us, Bill?" Jessie asked as we stepped into the lift. "Sad to say, there has been a fresh catnapping. The Lady Josephine Ashford-Sinclair's prized Persian, snatched in broad daylight from her Mayfair townhouse. No leads and a hefty ransom demand." Bill's brow furrowed. "The press has got wind of the cats we rescued from the warehouse and is now having a field day, dubbing it the 'Kitty Crime Wave.'"

George raised an eyebrow. "Rather sensationalist, don't you think?"

"Apt, though," I said. "A crime wave with actual waves - of fluff and whiskers!"

Jessie rolled her eyes good-naturedly as we exited the lift and made our way to Bill's temporary office. It had been made available on the orders of the Commissioner following the intervention of Lady Street-Walters who had been horrified to learn that the team were working from a cramped space in the Vauxhall lodging house.

Once inside the office, Jessie said, "We'll get to the bottom of this, Bill. Those catnapping fiends won't know what hit them."

George nodded and stroking his moustache said, "Indeed. We'll retrieve the purloined puss post-haste."

I hopped onto Bill's desk, my emerald eyes glinting. "Lead the way to Lady Josephine, my friends. This feline sleuth is ready to pounce on some clues!"

"Your enthusiasm is to be admired, Khan, but we must try to establish if this is the same gang or is it a copycat crime," Bill said.

"Very drôle, Bill," I said but Bill seemed puzzled. On reflection, I don't think Bill saw the funny side in what he had just said.

LADY JOSEPHINE ASHFORD-SINCLAIR'S MAYFAIR residence was a study in opulence, from the intricate plasterwork on the ceilings to the priceless art adorning the walls. The lady herself, a vision in silk and pearls, greeted the foursome, Isabel was now a fully-fledged member of the team, in her lavish drawing room.

"Oh, Detective Sergeant Roberts, I'm so grateful you're here," she trilled, her perfectly coiffed blonde hair bobbing as she spoke. "My darling Duchess Meowington snatched away! I'm utterly beside myself with worry."

Bill said, "We will do our utmost to recover your precious cat, Lady Ashford-Sinclair, this is Jessie Harper and her partner George Jenkins. They are specialist private investigators from Liverpool and this is their assistant, Isabel. Can you tell us more about Duchess Meowington's disappearance?"

As the socialite launched into her tale, George discreetly jotted notes in his leather-bound notebook. Jessie listened intently, her sharp mind deconstructing every detail for potential clues.

"...and then I found this dreadful note!" Lady Josephine produced a slip of paper with a trembling hand. "Demanding an absurd sum for her safe return. Oh, it's too terrible to contemplate!"

Jessie accepted the ransom note, examining it closely. "We'll do everything in our power to bring Duchess Meowington home safely, Lady Ashford-Sinclair. Now, can you think of anyone who might wish you or your cat harm? Any disgruntled staff or rivals, perhaps?"

"Nobody in their right mind would want to harm my precious cat," she said.

"And the ransom note... how was it delivered?" Bill said.

"The cook found it on the front doorstep early in the morning and brought it to my attention," the socialite said.

As they stepped out into the crisp London air, leaving Lady Ashford-Sinclair's opulent residence behind, Jessie and George fell into step beside each other. The comfortable silence stretched between them, broken only by the rhythmic tapping of George's cane against the paving stones.

Bill, Isabel and Khan followed a few yards behind until Jessie and George came to an abrupt halt.

Waiting for the others to join them in a pavement huddle, Jessie said, "Did anyone notice anything unusual about what Lady Ashford-Sinclair said?"

Isabel piped up immediately, "If you mean what she didn't say then yes, I did."

"Please continue, Isabel." Jessie said.

"You asked her 'can you think of anyone who might *wish you* or your cat harm' and that is a deliberate emphasis of 'wish you.'" Isabel said.

"Very good, now tell us why that is significant," Jessie said.

"She ignored the part about anyone wishing *her harm*."

"Exactly!"

"That's brilliant deduction, Isabel, but as always, we must keep an open mind about such things. There may be an innocent explanation why she failed to fully answer that question," Bill Roberts said.

Isabel beamed and her face took on the appearance of a beetroot. Sensing her face had turned bright red, Isabel said, "Forgive me. I am not used to such praise especially from the likes of you Sergeant Roberts."

"Tish-tosh! You deserve it," Bill said.

"So, are we saying this latest catnapping is not connected to the gang in Clerkenwell?" George said.

"Isabel, what do you think?" Jessie said.

"We don't know for sure. I believe we need to do some digging into Lady Ashford-Sinclair's background to help us answer that question."

"Splendid, that is your next task on our return to Scotland Yard," Jessie said.

With a contented purr, I hopped down from the street bench that I had used to watch the discussions between my human friends. I was ready to continue my own undercover investigation in the feline community. "Well, I'll leave you four to do your investigating. But don't dally too long—we have a gang in Clerkenwell to arrest and another stolen cat mystery to solve."

As I slipped away into the shadows, I couldn't help but smile.

The Next Day

I strutted into Bill's temporary office in New Scotland Yard, my tail held high, feeling quite pleased with myself. "I come bearing gifts of knowledge, my dear companions," I announced, leaping onto the table where Jessie and George were poring over their notes.

Jessie looked up, her eyes filled with curiosity. "What have you discovered, Khan?"

I settled myself on a stack of papers, casting a glance at their scattered evidence. "Well, well, well. It seems you two have been busy. But I've uncovered a juicy titbit that might just be the missing piece to this puzzle."

George leaned forward stroking his moustache. "Do tell, Khan. We're all ears."

"Ah, the benefits of being a cat in a world of humans," I purred. "You'd be surprised what secrets are shared when we felines gather. There's a hidden network of catnappers operating right under your noses in Clerkenwell."

Jessie and George exchanged a look of surprise. "Khan, tell us something we don't know," Jessie said a tad impatiently. "It's how to catch them is the task we now face."

I nodded, "Indeed. And from what I've gathered, they're a slippery bunch. That is why we didn't catch them at the warehouse. But with my inside knowledge and your detective skills, we might just have a chance at catching them.

I also discovered they use another warehouse for auctioning off their ill-gotten gains and the name of a pub where they spend their money. Both of those establishments are also in Clerkenwell."

George's brow furrowed as he processed the information. "This could be the break we've been looking for. We need to inform Bill Roberts immediately."

As if on cue, Bill Roberts entered the room, his presence commanding attention. "Inform me of what, exactly?"

Jessie quickly filled him in on Khan's revelation, her words tumbling out in an excited rush. Bill listened intently, "Clerkenwell, you say? We know from our previous experience when we rescued the cats that's a tricky area to navigate. We'll need to proceed with caution." He turned to Khan, a glimmer of respect in his eyes. "Good work, Khan. Your undercover skills are proving invaluable."

I preened under the praise, my fur puffing up with pride. "Just doing my part, Bill. We cats have a way of blending in and gathering information."

Jessie and George were already deep in discussion, mapping out potential strategies for infiltrating the catnapping network. Their voices overlapped, ideas bouncing back and forth in rapid succession.

"We could pose as potential buyers," George suggested, his eyes alight with the thrill of the hunt.

Jessie nodded, her mind whirring with possibilities. "Or maybe infiltrate their ranks, gain their trust from the inside."

As they continued to brainstorm, Bill and I exchanged a knowing look. The energy in the room was electric fuelled by the Jessie and George's shared passion for justice and the growing bond between the two detectives.

I hopped down from the table, weaving between their legs. "Whatever plan you devise, count me in. I've got a few tricks up my fur that might come in handy."

Jessie reached down to scratch behind my ears, a gesture of affection and appreciation. "We couldn't do this without you, Khan. Your bravery and cunning are invaluable."

As the team continued to strategize, I couldn't help but feel a sense of pride and belonging. We were a diverse bunch, even more so now Isabel was on board, united by a common goal and the unshakable belief that justice would prevail. The catnappers of Clerkenwell wouldn't know what hit them.

After much deliberation about a plan of attack, Bill made the final decision.

THE WAREHOUSE LOOMED BEFORE us, a hulking structure of brick and shadows. The air hung heavy with the scent of damp and the faint echoes of distant city life. I felt the bristle of anticipation along my spine as we approached, my senses heightened and alert.

Jessie and George moved in perfect sync, their footsteps near silent on the pavement. They exchanged a glance, a wordless communication born of trust and understanding. With a nod, they split off to flank the entrance, Bill following close behind with Isabel in tow.

I darted ahead, my lithe form slipping through the shadows like a wisp of smoke. The darkness was my ally, cloaking my presence as I scouted the perimeter for signs of danger.

Inside, the warehouse was a labyrinth of crates and machinery, the air thick with the musty scent of old wood and rusted metal. Shafts of moonlight cut through the high windows, casting an eerie glow across the cluttered space.

Jessie and George moved forward, their steps measured and cautious. Their eyes swept the room, searching for any sign of the catnappers or their feline captives. The silence was broken only by the soft whisper of their breaths and the occasional creak of ancient floorboards.

Bill and Isabel had now joined us and as the team ventured deeper into the warehouse, a flicker of movement caught my eye. I froze, my muscles tensed and ready to spring. Slowly, I crept forward, my nose twitching as I sought to identify the source of the disturbance.

"What is it, Khan?" Jessie whispered, her voice barely audible above the thudding of my own heartbeat.

I didn't respond immediately, my focus entirely consumed by the task at hand. Step by step, I inched closer to the shadowed recess where I had detected the movement. My eyes narrowed, my whiskers quivering with anticipation.

And then, in a flash of fur and claws, I pounced.

A startled yelp echoed through the warehouse as I collided with my target. We tumbled across the floor in a tangle of limbs, my claws scrabbling for purchase on the rough concrete.

"Khan!" George hissed, his voice tinged with both concern and exasperation. "What are you doing?"

I disentangled myself from my opponent and sat back on my haunches, smoothing my ruffled fur with a nonchalant lick of my paw. "Just securing our perimeter," I replied, gesturing with my tail to the trembling figure huddled against the wall.

Jessie approached, her eyes widening as she saw me guarding my dishevelled prey. "What's going on?" she gasped, kneeling beside the scrawny tabby. "What is this tabby doing here?"

"His name is Archie and he can tell you himself now I have enabled his communication patterns," I said.

Archie looked up at her, his eyes wide with fear. "I... I heard about the catnappings," he stammered. "I wanted to help, but I got lost and–"

His words were cut short by the sudden sound of footsteps echoing through the warehouse. Jessie and George exchanged a tense glance, their hands instinctively reaching for their concealed weapons – two heavy wooden coshes.

"We've got company," George murmured, his eyes probing the shadows. "Khan, get Archie to safety. Jessie, Bill and I will handle this. Isabel, are you okay with this?"

"In for a penny, in for a pound," Isabel said as she wielded an evil looking hat pin she had removed from her flamboyant hat.

"Good, stay close then," George said. "Khan, I said take Archie to safety."

I nodded, gently nudging Archie to his feet. "Stick to me like glue," I whispered, guiding him towards a nearby stack of crates.

As we slipped into the shadows, I heard the unmistakable click of a gun being cocked. My heart raced, my senses heightened by the surge of adrenaline coursing through my veins.

Peering around the edge of the crate, I watched as Jessie, George, Bill and Isabel moved into position, their backs pressed against opposite walls. The footsteps grew louder, the sound of multiple assailants approaching from all sides.

"We know you're here," a gruff voice called out, the words echoing through the cavernous space. "Come out with your hands up, and nobody gets hurt."

Jessie's eyes met George's, a silent conversation passing between them. Jessie silently gestured to tell Bill and Isabel to remain where they were. Then with a subtle nod at George, they sprang into action, their movements perfectly synchronized.

George stepped out from behind cover, his cane raised in a defensive stance. His cosh ready in the other hand. "I'm afraid we can't do that," he called out, his voice calm and steady. "We have some questions for you first."

The catnappers emerged from the shadows, their faces obscured by dark masks. They fanned out, surrounding Jessie and George in a menacing semicircle.

"You're in no position to be asking questions," the leader snarled, his gun trained on George's chest. "Now, drop your weapons and come quietly, or we'll–"

His words were cut short by a sudden blur of movement. Isabel had taken the gunman by surprise. She had launched herself forward with her hatpin at the ready sticking it hard into the gunman's hand. He screamed in pain and the gun clattered to the floor, skidding across the concrete. Isabel was more surprised than the gunman at her bravery in the face of immediate and present danger.

George sprang into action, his cane whirling through the air as he engaged the nearest catnapper. The sound of flesh impacting wood echoed through the warehouse as George landed a series of precise blows.

Jessie ducked and weaved, her fists a blur of motion as she fought off two assailants at once. Her hair had come loose from its bun, cascading down her back in a fiery wave. Bill and Isabel joined forces with Jessie repelling the two assailants.

I watched in awe, my tail twitching with excitement as my companions demonstrated their formidable skills. Beside me, Archie trembled, his eyes wide with a mixture of fear and admiration.

The fight was over almost as quickly as it had begun. The catnappers lay sprawled across the floor, groaning in pain as Jessie, George, Bill and Isabel stood over them, their chests heaving with exertion.

"Well," George said, straightening his tie with a wry smile. "That was invigorating."

Jessie laughed, the sound echoing through the warehouse like a melody. "Just another day at the office, dear."

"You may be laughing now but we will have the last laugh. Just watch your backs, you meddling fools," one of the catnappers said.

The team ignored him but made a mental note of what had been said.

As the adrenaline began to fade, I emerged from my hiding spot, Archie trailing behind me. Jessie knelt, scratching me behind the ears with a gentle hand.

"Good work, Khan," she murmured, her eyes shining with pride. "You kept Archie safe."

I purred, leaning into her touch. "All in a day's work," I replied, my voice tinged with satisfaction.

George approached, his cane tapping against the concrete. "We should call in reinforcements," he said, his expression serious. "There may be more of them out there."

Jessie nodded, rising to her feet. "Agreed. But first, let's make sure these ones are secure."

As they set about restraining the catnappers, I turned to Archie, my tail curling around his shoulders in a gesture of comfort.

"You did well, kid," I said, my voice softening. "It takes courage to stand up for what's right."

Archie looked up at me, his eyes wide with gratitude. "Thank you, Khan," he whispered, his voice trembling slightly. "I couldn't have done it without you."

I chuckled, giving him a gentle nudge with my nose. "Stick with me, kid. I'll teach you everything I know."

"Thanks, but no thanks. Life is too scary around you lot. I'll settle for the quiet life," Archie said.

As the sound of police car bells began to fill the air, I settled back on my haunches, watching as Jessie, George, Bill and Isabel worked as a team. They moved in perfect harmony, their actions speaking louder than words ever could.

In that moment, I knew that whatever challenges lay ahead, we would face them together. A team, united by our love for justice and our unwavering commitment to each other.

And as the first rays of dawn began to filter through the high windows, casting a golden glow across the warehouse floor, I felt a sense of peace settle over me. We had won this battle, but the war was far from over.

The drive back to Scotland Yard in a police van was filled with a mixture of exhaustion and anticipation. Jessie sat up front, her eyes fixed on the road ahead, while George sat beside her, his brow furrowed in deep thought.

I lounged in one of the backseats sitting next to Isabel, my tail flicking lazily as I watched the city streets pass by. The adrenaline from our narrow escape at the warehouse was starting to wear off, replaced by a bone-deep weariness that seemed to seep into every fibre of my being.

As we pulled up outside Scotland Yard, Jessie turned to face George, her hazel eyes searching his face. "What do you think that message could mean?" she asked, her voice low and urgent.

George shook his head, his expression pensive. "I don't know, Jessie. But whatever it is, we need to be prepared for anything."

They exchanged a look that spoke volumes, their eyes conveying a depth of understanding that went beyond mere words. In that moment, I could see the bond between them, the unbreakable connection that had been forged through countless hours of working side by side, facing danger and uncertainty together.

As they climbed out of the van, I leapt onto Jessie's shoulder, my claws digging into the soft wool of her coat. She reached up absently to scratch behind my ears, her mind already racing ahead to the challenges that lay before us.

Inside Bill's office, a clerk assigned to Bill looked up from her desk, her eyes widening at the sight of our dishevelled appearance. "What happened?" she asked, her voice laced with concern. On being ignored, she added, "There's a message for you here."

Having ignored her questions, Jessie said, "No time to explain now. We need to see that message."

The clerk nodded, her expression grave as she handed over a plain white envelope. Jessie tore it open with trembling fingers, her eyes scanning the contents quickly. The note read:

IF YOU VALUE YOUR LIVES GO BACK TO LIVERPOOL

As Jessie read, I could see the colour drain from her face, her lips pressing together in a tight line. Beside her, George leaned in closer, his own expression growing increasingly troubled as he read over her shoulder.

"What does it say?" I demanded, my tail lashing impatiently.

Jessie looked up, her eyes meeting mine with a mixture of determination and fear. "It's a warning," she said, her voice barely above a whisper. "Whoever is behind these catnappings, they know we're onto them. And they're not going to stop until they get what they want."

George placed a hand on her shoulder, his touch gentle but firm. "We'll figure this out, Jess. Together."

She nodded, taking a deep breath as she squared her shoulders. "You're right, G.J. We've come too far to give up now."

As they bent their heads together, poring over the message for any clues, I couldn't help but feel a surge of pride. These were my humans, brave and resourceful and utterly determined to see justice done.

Chapter Nine

Isabel walked to the lodging house in Vauxhall taking in the sights of London along the Embankment and marvelling at what she saw like many a thousand new visitors to the capital every week of the year.

On arrival Mrs Swarbrick gratefully accepted the four-weeks advance payment for the two rooms accommodating Isabel, Jessie, George and Bill Roberts. The two ladies used one and the two gentlemen used the other bedroom. Enjoying a cup of tea with Mrs Swarbrick and before leaving, Mrs Swarbrick said, "I almost forgot. There's a laundry bag out back with a note pinned to it addressed to Dale Street Private Investigations. I think it's for Jessie."

"Right, show me to it," Isabel said.

The landlady took Isabel out to the laundry room at the back of the building and pointed out a white laundry bag with a note attached to it. Isabel saw that the bag was lumpy as if it contained something. Reaching up, she grabbed the bag but first removed the note. On peering inside the bag, she found five dead rats.

Isabel recoiled in disgust and took some minutes to recover her composure then she read the note which said:

> *5 DEAD RATS. JESSIE GEORGE BILL AND ISABEL NOT FORGETTING KHAN GO BACK TO LIVERPOOL IF YOU DON'T WANT TO JOIN THESE RATS*

Pulling her handkerchief from her dress pocket, Isabel dabbed her eyes again composing herself quickly in the knowledge Mrs Swarbrick was watching her.

"May I use the telephone?" Isabel said.

"Of course, my dear," the landlady replied.

After dialling the Scotland Yard Whitehall 1212 number and asking for the office of Detective Sergeant Roberts she was connected and spoke with Jessie. Isabel poured out the story then there was a pause at the end of the line.

"Jessie, are you still there?" Isabel said.

"I am. Sorry I'm thinking... look... just ask Mrs Swarbrick if she saw anything unusual ideally a description of the vile person who left this filth," Jessie said. "And tell Mrs Swarbrick to leave the rats in the bag until George gets there to take a photograph. You can bring the note back with you though."

"Alright," Isabel said.

"Are you okay, my dear?" Jessie said.

"Fine," Isabel said but Jessie knew she was putting on a brave face.

Isabel followed her instructions then walked back to Scotland Yard.

The room used as Bill's office seemed to pulse with tension as the team waited for Isabel to finish her account.

"Mrs Swarbrick was adamant," Isabel said, "it was an off-duty police officer because he wasn't wearing his armband around his wrist. She also saw his collar number and it started with the letters CL which she says is Clerkenwell Division…"

"Wait, sorry to interrupt but how does she know all about armbands and collar numbers?" Bill asked.

"She has an uncle in the Metropolitan Police," Isabel gushed.

"Alright, but did she see this policeman with the laundry bag?" Bill said.

"No, but she said he was nervous and asked to look in the laundry room because he was chasing a miscreant. She didn't believe him because he wasn't out of breath but nevertheless allowed him into the laundry room alone." Isabel said.

"Isabel, thank you. You have done an excellent job," Bill said.

"What do you make of all this, Bill?" George said.

"I'm trying not to jump to the obvious conclusion that Detective Inspector Clement Ward is behind all this," Bill said rubbing his chin in thought. "It's an open secret I don't trust him and I believe he tried his best to sabotage our investigation on that first night he took us to Clerkenwell then disappeared leaving us exposed in roughhouse territory."

"If it is him then his information on what we are doing is bang up to date because Isabel is mentioned in that note," George said. "Come to think of it, it must be him as he's the only human outside of this team who knows about Khan and his magical abilities," Bill said.

"Hmm... that begs two questions: is there someone else involved as well as Ward? And is it safe for us to continue lodging at Mrs Swarbrick's," George said.

Jessie Harper's hands clenched into fists as she looked at George and Isabel, each of their faces etched with shock and disbelief.

"Impossible," Jessie muttered through gritted teeth, her voice barely more than a whisper. "How could we not have known?"

George's dark eyes were wide with surprise, his grip on his cane tightening. "I would never have suspected. We've been deceived by someone we thought we could trust."

Bill shook his head, his blue eyes clouded with betrayal. "It's like a dagger to the heart, it is. Never thought I'd see the day when our trust was so thoroughly broken especially by a police officer."

As the team stared at one another, their initial shock began to give way to anger and frustration. Jessie slammed her fist down on the table, causing the lamp to wobble precariously.

"Damn it!" she exclaimed. "We should have seen this coming! What kind of investigators are we if we can't even see through the lies of those closest to us?"

"Jessie, we can't blame ourselves for this," George said, his voice calm but strained. "We had no reason to suspect anything."

"Didn't we?" Bill said, his Welsh accent becoming more pronounced as his emotions flared. "There were signs, there must have been! How could we have been so blind?"

"Enough!" Jessie shouted, silencing both men. Her breaths came in short, sharp bursts as she tried to process the enormity of the situation. "Arguing won't change anything. We need to focus on what we do now."

"First, we need to find out how deep this betrayal goes," George suggested, his mind already working to untangle the web of deception. "There may be others involved, others we thought we could trust."

"George is right," Bill agreed reluctantly. "We can't afford to take anything for granted anymore. We need to question everything and everyone."

Jessie nodded, "We'll get to the bottom of this, no matter what it takes. And when we do, I swear, they'll pay for what they've done."

The room seemed to grow smaller as Jessie, George, Bill and Isabel each retreated into their thoughts. Jessie leaned against the wall, her gaze unfocused as she replayed recent events in her mind. How had they been so blind? She clenched her fists, her nails digging into her palms as she grappled with the bitter sting of betrayal.

"Jessie," George's voice broke through the silence, his brow furrowed with concern. "We can't let this consume us."

"George is right," Bill said, his voice heavy with fatigue. "If there are others involved, we need to focus on finding them. Sitting here dwelling on our own mistakes won't help anyone."

"Alright," Jessie agreed, straightening herself up. "Let's go over everything again. Maybe we missed something."

They gathered around a small table, its surface cluttered with notes and photographs. As they began discussing their suspicions, Jessie found herself unable to shake the nagging feeling that they were overlooking something crucial. They'd been betrayed once; how could they trust any of the information they'd gathered thus far?

"Khan mentioned someone named Smith when he was undercover," George said tapping his finger on the table. "Could be an alias, but it's worth looking into."

"Smith, eh?" Jessie's eyes narrowed as she considered the possibility. "It's common enough to be an alias, but we can't rule anything out at this point."

"True," Bill conceded.

"Right," George agreed. "We have to consider every possible connection. There may be a larger network involved in this catnapping scheme, and if there is, we need to take them down."

"Is it possible there are two gangs?" Isabel said.

"Why do you say that?" Bill said.

"Well. We know for sure about the gang in Clerkenwell because of the cats we rescued but what about this stuff about mystical creatures? Is it the catnappers also involved with that or a separate gang?" Isabel said.

"Good thinking, Isabel," George said.

"You might be right. We really cannot rule anything out yet," Jessie nodded, her determination returning. "As for the threats, we've been deceived once but we won't let it happen again. We will bring all those involved to justice and protect the innocent."

"Khan would be proud of you," George offered a small smile, his eyes reflecting the same resolve as Jessie's.

"Let's just hope we can live up to Khan's expectations," Bill muttered grimly, his gaze fixed on the notes scattered across the table. "Alright, then," Bill said. "Let's get to work. Together, we'll uncover the truth."

"Khan," Jessie said, her eyes wide with concern. "What if his undercover mission is at risk?"

"Damn," George muttered, running a hand through his hair. "We've been so focused on our own feelings that we forgot about Khan's safety."

"Right now, he's our most valuable source of information," Bill added. "But if the mastermind knows we're onto them, he could be in danger."

"Khan's clever, resourceful, and has an air of mystery around him," Jessie said, trying to reassure herself and the others. "I just hope he can stay hidden long enough for us to figure out our next move."

Jessie also thought, "I wish I could switch on our telepathic channel at will." But she knew it was Khan who controlled that.

"Can we trust him to continue gathering information, though?" George asked, weighing the risks. "If something goes wrong, we might lose our only chance at bringing down this catnapping ring."

"Khan trusts us," Jessie insisted, her voice unwavering. "And I trust him. We need to keep him involved but we have to find a way to minimise the risks."

"Agreed," Bill nodded solemnly. "For all we know, there could be eyes and ears everywhere. We need to watch our backs."

As if on cue, the investigators became hyper-aware of their surroundings. Every creak in the floorboards, every gust of wind rattling the windowpanes felt like potential threats lurking in the shadows.

"Let's review our findings so far," Jessie suggested, her voice barely above a whisper. "But first, let's make sure this room is secure."

George and Bill nodded in agreement, their faces etched with caution. Together, they checked for any possible signs of surveillance or recording devices - a task that once would have seemed paranoid but now felt necessary.

"Alright," George said after they had thoroughly inspected the room. "I think we're safe to talk freely. But let's keep our voices low, just in case."

"Khan has always been careful to communicate only in secure locations," Jessie began, her mind racing with worry for her feline friend. "We need to make sure he knows we're aware of the situation and that we're doing everything we can to protect him."

"Maybe we should establish a secret code or signal," Bill suggested, his eyes darting around the room as if expecting danger to appear at any moment. "Something subtle that would allow us to relay messages without arousing suspicion."

"Good idea," George agreed, his voice strained with tension. "We'll work on it together. The more precautions we take, the better."

As they huddled closer, conspiring in hushed voices, each investigator knew that the stakes were higher than ever. Trust had been broken, lives were on the line, and every move they made could either bring them closer to justice or plunge them deeper into peril. But with Khan's safety hanging in the balance, they couldn't afford to falter. They had to remain vigilant and resolute, navigating the treacherous waters of deception and betrayal to uncover the truth - and protect those they held dear.

With a soft clink, Jessie, George, Bill and Isabel joined their raised teacups in unison. "To justice," they whispered, steeling themselves for the confrontation ahead.

"Let's go bring these catnappers down," Jessie said, her eyes gleaming as she set her cup down on the table. She grabbed her coat and hat, ready to track down and face the mastermind behind the cruel operation.

"Jessie, before we go, remember that whoever we're up against is cunning, ruthless, and has already deceived us once," George cautioned, adjusting his homburg hat. "We must be prepared for anything."

"Agreed," Bill chipped in, his voice steady but betraying a hint of nerves. "But together, we can outsmart them."

"Where do we sleep tonight?" Jessie said.

"Same as usual. We shouldn't give in to intimidation tactics," Bill said, "everyone agreed?"

"Aye, aye," was the chorus of approval.

As the team walked through the streets of 1930s London, each investigator felt the weight of their mission pressing down on their shoulders. They kept their senses sharpened, alert to any possible threats lurking in the shadows. The tension was palpable, and Jessie could practically hear the pounding of her own heart in her ears.

"Khan would've loved this," Jessie thought, allowing herself a fleeting smile amidst the gravity of the situation. "His wit and resourcefulness would have been invaluable here."

Her thoughts were interrupted by a police car that pulled up alongside the team. A man in a suit got out of the car and approached them. Showing his identification, he said, "I'm Detective Constable Ernie Wise and I have an urgent message for you."

"What is it, lad," Bill said with more than a hint of suspicion.

"My guvnor, DI Ward wants to see you urgently. He says he can show you where the catnappers are right now."

"How do we know this is all above board?" Bill said.

"Please yourselves. I'm only the messenger."

"Okay. Okay. Where is Ward now?" Bill said.

The detective handed over a scribbled map showing the location of a warehouse in Alie Street, Aldgate East and instructions as to how to get there by catching an eastbound District Line train to Aldgate East.

Once he had handed over the note, the detective got back in the police car and left.

During the following brief team discussion on the pavement, caution was thrown to the wind. As Bill succinctly put it, "What do we have to lose?"

Jessie thought, "Khan might have said, 'Your lives.' Then again, he might not have said anything."

Upon reaching the entrance to a seedy warehouse in Alie Street, they paused for a moment, taking a deep breath before pushing open the door. Inside, they found themselves face-to-face with the gang leader who it seemed had been waiting for their arrival. This person was standing in the shadows - someone they had once trusted.

"Surprised to see us?" Jessie spat, her voice dripping with contempt and betrayal.

"Ah, Jessie, always so perceptive," the leader sneered, smirking at their stunned expressions. "You were such useful pawns." As he stepped forward out of the shadows Jessie, George and Bill were shocked to see that the man in front of them was not who they expected.

"Who are you?" Jessie said.

"Derek Kray. I'm DI Ward's detective sergeant at Clerkenwell Division. You stupid fools thought it was Ward behind the catnapping ring when it was me all along pulling the strings. You were all like puppets in my play. Ward was a stupid pawn too, telling me everything I needed to know about what you were up to. He had access to your office at the Yard, did you know that?"

Ignoring that and as cool as a cucumber, Bill said, "Tell us this... was your gang responsible for stealing Lady Ashford-Sinclair's Siamese?"

"Who? Never heard of her. Now shut up," Kray said.

"Enough!" George barked, stepping forward. "We know what you've done, and we're here to put an end to it."

"Good luck with that," Kray taunted, signalling to a group of burly henchmen who emerged from the shadows. "You'll never get past my associates."

Jessie's mind raced as she assessed the situation. Outnumbered and outmatched, they needed to think fast. She exchanged a glance with George, Bill and Isabel, each of them silently acknowledging their mutual understanding - it was now or never.

"Time for Plan B," Jessie murmured under her breath as she feigned a stumble, drawing the attention of one of the henchmen. Seizing the opportunity, Bill launched into action, disarming another henchman with a swift, expert move whilst Isabel went into an attacking frenzy with her hatpin in her hand.

"Khan would be proud," Jessie thought as she watched George use his cane to trip up a charging adversary. Despite the odds stacked against them, their teamwork and quick thinking were turning the tide in their favour.

As the last henchman fell, stabbed in the neck by Isabel, Kray realised they had been outsmarted. Cornered and defeated, he could do nothing but glare at the foursome with bitter resentment.

"Justice always prevails," Jessie said coolly, her voice steady and triumphant as she watched Bill handcuff Kray to a radiator pipe.

"You're going nowhere, Kray," Bill said.

"Khan," Jessie whispered, looking skyward, "we did it."

"SIT DOWN, EVERYONE. WE need to regroup," Jessie said, her voice hoarse but steady as she led George, Bill and Isabel into a small, dimly lit room. They collapsed onto the worn furniture, their bodies aching from the exertion of their recent confrontation.

"Blimey, I never thought we'd get out of that one," Bill admitted, rubbing his bruised knuckles. "But we did it, didn't we? Put a stop to those bloody catnappers."

"Indeed, we did," George agreed, leaning back in his chair with a sigh. "But at what cost? Was discovering a betrayal worth it?"

Jessie's expression darkened at the mention of the betrayal they had experienced. It was hard to swallow that someone they thought they could initially trust had a key part in the catnapping operation, and a police officer. Indeed, the boss was also another police officer. "We'll deal with it," she said firmly. "For now, let's focus on how we can wrap up this investigation and make sure justice is served."

The team exchanged determined looks, drawing strength from their shared experiences.

"Khan would have been proud of us today," Bill remarked, a glimmer of a smile appearing on his face. "I wish he were here to celebrate our victory."

"Me too," Jessie murmured, her thoughts turning to their magical companion. She knew Khan was still undercover, gathering valuable information about the possibility of a larger network operating besides the catnapping scheme. She couldn't help but worry about his safety, especially after the betrayal they had suffered. "He always knows what to say to lighten the mood," she added, a wistful smile gracing her lips.

"Speaking of Khan," George began, his voice softening, "we need to discuss what we've learned from this ordeal.

The betrayal... it has changed everything. How do we move forward knowing that we were deceived by someone in a position of authority?"

"By not letting it break us," Jessie replied. "We learn from it and we use that knowledge to become even more vigilant in our work."

"Indeed," Bill said. "We can't let one betrayal define us or weaken our resolve. We must adapt and continue to seek the truth, no matter how difficult it may be."

"Khan would say something witty right about now," Jessie said, allowing a small smile to play at the corners of her mouth. "He'd remind us that we're stronger together and that we've faced worse obstacles before."

"True," George said, his eyes reflecting a mix of determination and sadness. "We owe it to ourselves and those we serve to see this investigation through to the end."

"Right," Jessie agreed, her voice steady and strong. "Let's finish what we started, for Khan, for all those innocent cats, and for justice."

"Now. Let's take Kray to the police station and find him a nice, cold cell," Bill said.

Later, as the team thoroughly dissected recent events, Jessie, George, Bill and even Isabel as a newcomer, found solace in their shared experience and the lessons they had learned from recent events. They knew they could face any challenge that lay ahead bolstered by their camaraderie and the knowledge that they could overcome even the most unexpected obstacles. As they prepared to delve back into the shadows of their investigation, they carried with them the spirit of their absent friend, Khan – his wit, wisdom, and unwavering loyalty serving as an enduring reminder of the strength they drew from one another.

One Week Later

Jessie, George, Bill and Isabel stood together at a small ceremony organised by Lady Street-Walters and the Mayfair Rotary Club to honour their successful efforts in solving the catnapping case. The setting sun painted amber hues across the faces of the attendees, warming the atmosphere as they gathered around the foursome.

"Jessie," George began, his voice filled with pride, "I just wanted to say how grateful I am for all your hard work during this investigation. We couldn't have done it without you."

"Likewise, George," Jessie replied, her eyes shining with appreciation. "Your dedication and resourcefulness were invaluable. And Bill, thank you for guiding us when we needed you most. Not forgetting you, Isabel for becoming a valued member of the investigations team of Dale Street Private Investigations Agency."

"Ah, it was nothing," Bill said modestly, scratching the back of his head. "I just did what I could to help. Isabel was the real star."

"Here's to many more successful cases with the Dale Street Private Investigations Agency," Jessie said, raising an imaginary toast.

The four of them exchanged warm smiles, basking in the shared sense of accomplishment and camaraderie that had grown stronger throughout their investigation. They knew that they could rely on each other in the face of any challenge, and that the trust between them was unbreakable.

As the team continued to receive congratulations from various community members, I decided to make an appearance but remaining invisible to all save for my human colleagues. I weaved my way between people's legs before coming to a stop at Jessie's feet.

"Ah, there you are," Jessie said, bending down to scratch behind my ears. "We were just talking about our accomplishments."

"Indeed," I purred, "and while I applaud your achievements, I can't help but remember a certain incident involving a rather clumsy attempt at tailing a suspect. If memory serves me correctly, Mr Jenkins, you managed to knock over not one, but two rubbish bins in the process."

George flushed with embarrassment, recalling the debacle. "Well, sorry that we are not all as slinky as you, Khan," he said good-naturedly.

"Fortunately for us all, I don't need to rely on such primitive methods," I said smugly, flicking my tail. "In any case, I believe it's high time we returned to our regular duties at the agency. After all, there are plenty of mysteries waiting to be solved."

Jessie chuckled and glanced at the team, their faces now alight with laughter. In this moment of levity, they found solace in their bond as they prepared to face whatever challenges awaited them at the Dale Street Private Investigations Agency. But first, Jessie knew there was unfinished business here in London.

"Just hold on there, my feline friend, we still have work to do here," Jessie said.

"New mission, old habits," I said cryptically as I stared out into space.

"We must get to the bottom of the mystery behind these magical creatures," Jessie said.

"We must. I agree," George said, leaning on his cane as he studied the sea of faces come to congratulate them on cracking the catnapping caper.

"Quite right," I said, "let me say I was simply testing your determination to see this thing through to the end. "Otherwise, one might say our tenacity rivals that of a certain investigator who once attempted to scale a drainpipe in pursuit of a thief only to be thwarted by an ill-timed sneeze."

"Khan!" Jessie exclaimed, her cheeks flushing with embarrassment while George chuckled. "That was one time, and I thought we agreed never to speak of it again."

"Ah, but where's the fun in keeping such an entertaining tale to myself?" I replied with a sly grin.

"Alright, enough reminiscing," George intervened, a hint of amusement still lingering in his voice. "We need to focus on what lies ahead. The mastermind behind the catnapping operation may be gone, but this larger conspiracy is far from over."

"George is right," Jessie agreed, her expression turning serious. "We must stay vigilant and trust our instincts. We've come too far to let anything stand in our way now."

"Indeed," I added solemnly. "And though the path before us may be fraught with danger, I know that together, we are more than capable of overcoming any obstacle."

"Here's to the Dale Street Private Investigations Agency," George said, raising an imaginary glass in toast.

"Here's to us," Jessie said, "and to uncovering the truth, no matter where it leads."

As the team prepared for the next chapter of their investigation, they drew strength from the bond that had formed between them. United by trust, loyalty, and a shared sense of purpose, they were ready to face whatever challenges awaited them – and to bring the larger conspiracy involving magical creatures to light.

Chapter Ten

I SLINKED THROUGH THE narrow alleys of Clerkenwell planning my strategy. The guise of a common stray was beneath me but necessities were necessities when on an undercover operation. I now fitted in looking like a scrawny feral alley cat. Somewhere amongst these dilapidated brick buildings and the pungent scent of refuse, a den of thieves lurked snatching up my fellow creatures for their deplorable schemes.

"Oi, new face," a tabby with a notched ear called out, eyeing me from atop a dustbin. "What's your story?"

"Simply a traveller seeking temporary refuge," I replied, my voice casual but confident. "The streets are unforgiving for a lone feline."

"True enough," the tabby conceded with a flick of his tail. "Name's Scraps. You got a handle, stranger?"

"Khan," I said, and then added with a hint of dry humour, "The Enigmatic Feline."

"Enigmatic, eh?" Scraps chuckled. "You'll fit right in here. Lots of enigmas in Clerkenwell, including why anyone would bother stealing that yowling lot down the way."

"Stealing, you say?" I feigned nonchalance even as my emerald eyes glinted with interest. "An intriguing predicament indeed."

"Indeed," Scraps mimicked, rolling his eyes. "Been a regular catnapping spree. They don't nab the likes of us, though. Too street-smart, we are. Anyways, they got nicked by some out of town cop and private eyes. Now another gang has moved in but they ain't interested in ordinary cats, pedigree or otherwise."

"Of course," I said as if this was common knowledge and letting my gaze wander nonchalantly. My magical abilities allowed me to sense things beyond the ordinary—a whiff of enchantment here, a ripple of ill intent there. These abilities were key in blending into the feline tapestry of London's underbelly.

It looked like my new friend was about to leave so I asked him a burning question, "If they're not cats making that racket, what are they?"

"All kinds, mate. Creatures that'll fetch a fair penny at auction. They're erotic, you see," Scraps said.

I tried hard not to laugh but failed.

"Oi! What's funny?" Scraps said looking wounded.

"Nothing. I see what you mean about exotic creatures. I think that's a peacock making that noise like a trumpet," I said.

"Yeah, exotic... bloody noisy too," Scraps said. "Anyway, keep your ears perked, Khan," he advised before leaping off the bin and sauntering away.

"Perked and primed," I assured him, though he was already out of earshot. With a subtle shift of my posture, I activated the magic coursing under my fur, fine-tuning my senses to pick up the subtleties of conversation and movement around me.

As I prowled the community, it wasn't long before I picked up the threads of whispered plans and furtive glances. I moved with purpose, yet with the languid grace of any cat with no particular place to be. There were mentions of a shipment, a collection, a profit to be made—all cloaked in the coded language of those who preferred their dealings to remain discreet.

"Sounds like someone's been dipping their paws into forbidden cream," I thought with a smirk. If there was one thing I relished more than a good nap in the sun, it was unravelling the tangled skeins of a mystery.

I continued to observe, my mind cataloguing each useful snippet of information. Descriptions of humans with shifty eyes and greed-lined pockets, locations exchanged with a nod and a twitch, all while I pretended to groom my whiskers or chase a particularly audacious rat that had crossed my path.

"Ah, the life of an enigmatic feline," I sighed theatrically to no one in particular, "is never dull."

With the gathered intelligence woven securely in my mental tapestry, I knew it was time to retreat and regroup with Jessie, George, Bill and Isabel. They'd need to hear about the murmurings of mischief in Clerkenwell. After all, every good detective—whether covered in fur or not—knows the importance of sharing clues with one's allies. And perhaps, just perhaps, I'd share my latest escapade with a touch of dramatic flair worthy of a cat of my mystical standing.

As I thought about the piece of drama to use to announce my findings to the team, I continued to saunter nonchalantly along cobblestone paths and ancient alleyways once the province of highwaymen. My tail was high and eyes alert, blending seamlessly with the shadows of Clerkenwell. The muffled din of the human world faded into a distant hum, leaving only the nocturnal symphony of the city's feline inhabitants to fill my keen ears.

"Oi, Whiskers," called out a scrappy tabby with a missing ear, addressing a sleek grey cat lounging atop a dustbin, "you comin' to the big meet tonight?"

"Wouldn't miss it for the world," replied Whiskers with an air of mystery. "Heard it's at the old warehouse on Cutter's Row."

"Right, right. Keep it under your hat, though," the tabby added with a conspiratorial glance. "You know how they are about secrecy."

"Under my hat?" I thought, stifling a chuckle. "If I wore one, it'd be purely for stylistic purposes. But this information—now that's something to keep tucked behind the ol' ear." He made a point of scratching his neck, as if chasing a flea, while his mind raced with possibilities.

"Thanks for the tip," I meowed softly, but the other cats were too wrapped up in their own conversation to pay him any heed. "Now, to find this mysterious gathering."

The night grew darker as I made my way through the narrow streets, my silent paws carrying me towards Cutter's Row. The dilapidated warehouse loomed ahead, its skeletal frame a stark silhouette against the London sky. With the agility of a creature born to navigate the night, I slipped through a gap in the fence and crept closer to the building.

"Here we are," I murmured, peering through a cracked window. "Clerkenwell's very own den of iniquity."

With a flicker of magical energy that tingled through my whiskers, I embraced the shadows that clung to the corners of the warehouse. My body contorted, bones reshaping, fur receding—a sensation not unpleasant, akin to the stretch after a long nap. In moments, where once there was a cat, now stood a mouse, modest in size but unparalleled in stealth.

"Let's see how they like this little game of cat and mouse," I thought with a chuckle that came out as an imperceptible squeak.

My newfound form afforded me access to the nooks and crannies of the warehouse, skittering behind crates and weaving between boots much larger than my entire body. From this vantage point, I could gather the information Jessie and George needed without raising an alarm.

"Remember, the next shipment comes at midnight," a gruff-voiced man commanded, unaware of the tiny intruder eavesdropping. "And Harvey, make sure those cages are secure. We can't afford any... mishaps."

"Harvey? Secure?" I resisted the urge to laugh aloud—or squeak, rather. If Harvey's grasp on security was anything like his understanding of personal hygiene, we'd have nothing to worry about.

"Midnight, cages, Harvey's incompetence," I listed mentally, filing away each detail. "This is almost too easy."

I was close enough now to see the grime beneath their fingernails, the flecks of spit that flew from their mouths as they spoke. But even as I gathered their secrets, I felt the tug of my true nature. A cat in a mouse's costume was still a cat at heart.

"Time to wrap this up," I decided, whiskers quivering with anticipation. "Jessie and George will want to hear about this—and I do enjoy being the bearer of good news. Or bad news. Really, any news that lets me show off."

With the gang's plan committed to memory, I retreated to the shadows once more. The transformation back into my feline form was smooth, a reversal of the enchantment that left me feeling whole again—and smugly satisfied with my evening's work.

"Brace yourselves," I murmured, picturing Jessie's determined face and George's often bemused expression. "Khan's coming home with a tale to tell."

It was then I heard the shout, "Harvey! You've let that black cat escape, you idiot!" It was gruff voice.

I had no idea if they were talking about me so - flash! Bang! I did a rapid costume change back into Mighty Mouse.

I skittered along the edge of the warehouse, my mousey form an inconspicuous whisper against the dusty floorboards. The thrill of the hunt—or in this case, the infiltration—raced through my tiny heart. A peculiar scent teased my whiskers, drawing me towards a seemingly innocuous section of the wall. Pressing my rodent nose to a crack, I sensed it: magic, old and powerful.

"Ah, hidden doors. How dreadfully hackneyed," I thought. Yet, I couldn't deny a surge of excitement as the wall slid open at the touch of a grimy paw—the not-so-secure security measure evidently overlooked by our dear friend Harvey.

Inside, another transformation from mouse to cat was swift, shadows wrapping around me like a cloak. As Khan once again, I prowled into the secret room. It was a menagerie of the mystical, a prison of impossibilities. Creatures of all shapes and sizes peered back at me with eyes that held the flicker of intelligence—and the dull sheen of defeat.

"Captivity doesn't suit you, chums," I whispered, though they could not understand. A pang of sympathy struck me; we were kin of a sort, bound by our otherworldliness.

"Quiet!" hissed a voice, jarring me from my thoughts. "The boss said we gotta keep 'em under wraps until the auction."

"Right, right. 'Cause magic fetches a pretty penny these days," another replied, scratching behind a greasy ear.

"Especially talking animals like that black cat the copper told us about," one of the gang said, gesturing wildly with a sausage-like finger. "Imagine what the high rollers will pay for that at auction!"

"Indeed, now which cop are they referring to? Kray or Ward?" I murmured, green eyes narrowing. "Imagine their disappointment when they find out I'm not for sale."

Their conversation continued, each word a sharpened blade aimed at the heart of my newfound comrades-in-cages. Exploit magical creatures for personal gain? Not on my watch. Or Jessie's. Or George's, for that matter. Not to mention Bill or Isabel.

"Time to conjure up a storm," I resolved, already plotting our next move. The gang would have to be more than bumbling crooks and hapless Harveys to pull one over on us—a cat with secrets, a red-headed Welshman, a sartorial disaster of a receptionist cum detective, a woman sleuth with courage and a business partner with... well, George had many attributes, bless him.

"Your nefarious plans are about to hit a snag, gents," I vowed silently. With that, I slipped away, unseen—a shadow amongst shadows, a whisper of justice on the wind.

It was then I heard more voices. I made myself invisible as this was getting tricky. My whiskers twitched in the dim light of the warehouse as I slinked from the shadows, my sleek black form barely distinguishable from the crates and debris littering the floor. I settled behind a rickety bookshelf, a relic from a forgotten office now repurposed as a lookout post. My attention was locked onto the group assembled before me.

"Right then," Khan whispered to himself, "time to play scribe."

The gang was an eclectic mix, each with a role clear as day. There was 'Fingers' Malone, adept at pickpocketing and petty theft; 'Bulldog' Brannigan, muscle through and through; and finally, 'Slick' Sammy, who seemed to have the gift of the gab, smooth-talking his way through deals and double-crosses. One by one, Khan committed their faces and foibles to memory. Fingers had a nervous tick, Bulldog winced at loud noises, and Slick... well, Slick had a penchant for waxing lyrical about his own brilliance—a vulnerability ripe for exploitation. Harvey and Gruff Voice were guarding the cages.

As if on cue, the gang stopped talking and in the case of Slick, stopped bragging, as the warehouse doors creaked open spilling a shaft of moonlight that cut across the dust motes dancing in the air. A figure stepped into the threshold, cloaked in mystery and an actual cloak, which seemed rather dramatic given the setting.

"Evening, chaps," came a voice cool as the night itself. The gang members straightened up, deference painted onto their grizzled faces.

"Boss," they mumbled in unison, like schoolboys caught passing notes instead of potions.

"Here we go," Khan muttered, "showtime."

"Been listening to your prattle," the Boss said, pacing with a swagger that suggested he owned more than just the room. "You lot think you're running the Ritz? This is serious business!"

"Of course, Boss," Slick Sammy stammered, his slickness slipping noticeably. "We've got top-quality magical creatures here, prime for the—"

"Silence!" The Boss snapped, and even the rats in the rafters seemed to hold their breath. "I didn't come here to listen to sales pitches. I want results. And none of your tomfoolery will mess this up, understand?"

Khan watched, ears perked, as Fingers shuffled uncomfortably and Bulldog's eyes darted to the exit. The hierarchy was clear: The Boss was the alpha, and the goons were the underlings prone to infighting and mishap. The perfect storm for a cat with a plan.

"Understood, boss," Bulldog growled, his tone suggesting that confrontation was the last thing he wanted.

"Good." The Boss nodded sharply. "Because if you fail me, it won't be the authorities you'll need to worry about—it'll be me. Am I making myself crystal?"

"Crystal, Boss," they chorused, though Khan noted how Bulldog's voice wavered like a candle in a tempest.

"Good, because you all know what happened to the toffs. Everyone thinks they did themselves in but we know better," the Boss said.

"Excellent, he must be referring to those socialites who took their own lives or so it seemed." I purred to no one in particular, my tail swishing with amusement. "Nothing like a bit of internal gang strife to stir the pot."

With the meeting dissolving into hushed planning and furtive glances, I knew it was time to withdraw, my mind a treasure trove of names and foibles of the gang members. But not before bestowing upon the scene a final, parting quip.

"Cheerio, gents," I whispered, as quiet as a secret and twice as enigmatic. "Do try not to bungle it up before we get our claws in, yeah?"

And with that, I vanished into the labyrinth of London's streets, a spectral agent of mischief and retribution, ready to share my findings with Jessie and George. The game, it seemed, was most definitely afoot.

"Khan has left the building," I announced to the empty alleyway as I made my escape, my feline form blending into the London night. "And he's bringing down the house."

I slipped away from the warehouse, my form a mere whisper of shadow against the grimy brickwork. The chill of the London night nipped at my sleek black fur as I navigated the maze of alleys with an ease born of feline instinct and supernatural cunning.

"Careful does it," I said, sidestepping a broken bottle—an unwitting alarm system for anyone clumsy enough to disturb it. "Wouldn't want to end this delightful escapade with unsightly scrapes."

It wasn't long before I arrived at Bill's office at Scotland Yard where the team of four awaited. They were huddled around a modest desk lamp, the golden glow casting shadows on their determined faces. Their eyes turned toward me as I leapt onto the desk and batted a moth away from the lamp.

"Finally," Jessie said. "What did you find?"

"Ah, the welcome I deserve," I said hopping down to the floor. "Gather 'round, my intrepid companions, for I bring tidings most dire and yet, curiously thrilling."

"Please get to the point, Khan," George urged, his moustache twitching with barely contained impatience. "What's the situation?"

"Very well," I acquiesced, jumping onto the desk again, my tail curling with dramatic flair. "The gang's plotting to exploit our fellow magical creatures—the sheer audacity! They're using them for personal gain, conducting business like a twisted menagerie."

"Magical creatures?" Bill Roberts echoed, his grizzled features tightening. "How many are we talking about?"

"Let's just say if they were to form a choir, the cacophony would be quite noteworthy," I replied with a wry tilt of my head.

"Exploitation of magical creatures... This is bigger than we thought," Jessie said, her gaze sharpening. "We have to stop them."

"Indeed," I agreed. "Their intentions are as dark as the underside of a newt, and twice as slippery."

"Any ideas on how we can take them down?" George asked, leaning on his cane, his mind already whirring into action.

"Several," I purred, relishing the anticipation in their eyes. "But first, we need to understand the full scope of their villainy. They've got names, roles, and deliciously exploitable weaknesses—all neatly catalogued up here." I tapped my head with a paw.

"Good work, Khan," Jessie praised, her voice warm with admiration. "You've given us exactly what we need to start unravelling their scheme."

"Unravelling—like a ball of yarn," I joked, unable to resist. "Oh, the metaphors abound!"

"Let's focus," George chided gently, though a smile played at the corners of his mouth. "We've got a lot of work ahead of us."

"Work that will undoubtedly benefit from my feline expertise and devilish charm," I added, stretching out across the desk basking in the glow of my own brilliance.

"Of course, Khan," Jessie said with a laugh, the tension in the room dissipating like mist. "Where would we be without you?"

"Perish the thought," I chuckled. "Now, let's craft a plan so cunning it would make a fox take notes."

As they all leaned in, forming a circle of conspirators illuminated by the steadfast lamp, I knew we were ready.

As I paced back and forth atop the worn mahogany desk, my fur shimmering in the lamplight, Jessie watched me with an amused tilt of her head, while George rested a hand on his chin, looking thoughtfully at me. I was listening to the plans being hatched by Bill and Isabel. They paused as if they knew something was on my mind. There was a brief silence.

"Something's not sitting right," I said breaking the silence, "DI Ward. He's been sniffing around this case like a hound with a bone, but I can't help suspecting he's chasing his own tail—or perhaps wagging it for someone else."

Jessie's brow furrowed, "But Kray said Ward was simply a pawn in the catnapping ring. So, you think Ward's involved in the mystical creatures' caper? That's a serious accusation, Khan."

"Observe, dear Jessie," I said in a tone that made them pay attention. "Ward's always one step behind, or so he claims. In fact, we have not seen nor heard from him for ages. But what if he's orchestrating a merry dance, ensuring we're always one step ahead of nothing?"

"Could be he's just bad at his job," George offered, though the note of scepticism in his voice suggested he considered Khan's theory plausible.

"Or good at pretending to be," I said, leaping down from the desk and beginning to weave between their legs. "We need a strategy—a plan that will outsmart them and expose their underhanded dealings with these poor creatures."

"Right," George agreed, standing up decisively. "We've got the element of surprise on our side. They don't know we're onto them, not fully. We could use that."

"Exactly, my dear Watson—figuratively speaking," I joked, tail flicking with satisfaction. "We'll lay a trap so subtle, it would make a spider applaud."

"Let's hear it then, Khan," Jessie said, her voice tinged with the thrill of the chase. "What's your grand plan?"

"Simple," I said, jumping back onto the desk with a grace only a cat could muster. "We play the game of shadows. They won't see us coming until it's too late. We'll infiltrate their clandestine meeting tonight, gather solid evidence, and have them arrested before the clock strikes midnight."

"Sounds risky," Bill Roberts said, leaning against the doorframe with a worried expression.

"Any clue as to what this meeting is about?" Jessie asked.

"It's clear to me it's the auction," I said, "and as for risk, Bill, isn't life a risk?" I replied sagaciously. "But fear not! With careful coordination and a dash of my supernatural stealth, we shall prevail."

"Alright, team," Jessie said, "let's get to work. We've got another gang to catch and more creatures to save."

"Remember," I added, my tone softening slightly, "we must tread lightly. The fate of those magical beings depends on our success. And, possibly, so does the integrity of Scotland Yard if Ward is indeed playing both sides."

"Then let's not disappoint them," George said rolling up his sleeves. "Or ourselves."

"Indeed," I purred, "Tonight, we make our move."

I swished my tail with a mischievous glint in my emerald eyes as I surveyed the room. The team's faces reflected a blend of anticipation and anxiety, a cocktail of emotions that always seemed to bubble up before any storm. Bill's brow was furrowed so deeply, one could hide a coin in the crevices.

"Ah, I see we're all a bundle of nerves," I said, leaping onto a stack of papers with the elegance of a dancer. "Let me ease your minds with a tale from my kitten days."

Jessie leaned back in her chair, arms crossed over her chest, a smile teasing her lips. "This ought to be good."

"Indeed," George said as his features relaxed. The man could out-stare a statue, but even he wasn't immune to my charms.

"Picture this," I started, voice rich with nostalgia. "Ancient Egypt, a land of sand and secrets. There I was, a young feline of no particular consequence, roaming the markets of Memphis near the great temple of Ptah."

"Memphis?" Bill said, scepticism knitting his bushy eyebrows. "As in Memphis, Tennessee?"

"Bill, my dear fellow, do try to keep up," I chided gently. "There is another Memphis, far older and more mysterious than its American namesake. Now, where was I? Ah, yes, the bustling market."

"Full of spices and silks, no doubt," Jessie said, playing along.

"Exactly!" Khan purred. "I found myself amidst the finest merchants, each peddling their wares with the gusto of an orator. And there, in the midst of it all, was a merchant who claimed he had a charm that could turn the most timid mouse into the fiercest lion."

"Did it work?" George asked, a hint of amusement in his voice.

"I was incredulous, of course," I continued. "But curiosity, as they say, killed the cat—or at least it would have liked to. I watched as a tiny mouse hesitantly approached the stall. The merchant, with a flourish worthy of a pharaoh, bestowed upon the rodent his magical charm."

"And?" Bill demanded, now fully engaged.

"The mouse puffed up, bold as brass, and marched directly toward the nearest cat—a rather large specimen with a reputation for terrorising the local vermin. The crowd held their breath, expecting a massacre."

"Let me guess," Jessie chuckled. "The mouse roared?"

"Indeed," I said, pausing for effect. "But not at the cat. Oh no. It turned its newfound courage on the merchant and demanded a refund for the lack of actual transformation!"

Laughter erupted around the office, breaking the tension like a hammer through glass. Even Bill's square jaw twitched in reluctant mirth.

"Point being," I concluded with a whisker-twitching smile, "sometimes the smallest among us can surprise the most daunting adversary. Much like us tonight."

"Here's to being courageous mice," Jessie raised an imaginary glass, her spirits visibly lifted.

"Cheers to that," George agreed, his eyes sparkling with humour.

"May our roar echo through Clerkenwell," I declared.

Chapter Eleven

The team of four and Khan, wasted no time in making their way back to the Clerkenwell warehouse where Khan had found the gang and the captive exotic creatures.

Khan made himself invisible and the others entered the auction room of the warehouse under cover of darkness. Jessie adjusted the brim of her hat, a necessary accessory to her disguise, as she glanced across the crowded room at George. Even with the homburg hat perched on his head and leaning slightly on his cane for effect, George's keen eyes missed nothing. They were inside the illicit auction venue, a place that reeked of wealth and dishonest dealings. This was far from the honest bustle of the Liverpool docklands they were accustomed to.

"Bit gaudy for my taste," Jessie murmured under her breath, eyeing the velvet drapes and golden trims that adorned the walls. Decorations that were in stark contrast to the rest of the warehouse.

"Quite," George said in a hushed tone, his gaze sweeping over the dimly lit room. The chandeliers, ornate and dripping with crystals, cast a subdued glow on the attendees, their faces partially masked by shadows and intrigue.

"Shh, you two," Isabel hissed from Jessie's other side, her voice barely audible above the soft music that filled the air with a haunting melody. "You're supposed to be buyers, not critics."

Bill Roberts, standing a head taller than most in the crowd, gave a curt nod from where he was positioned near a pillar, his sharp eyes searching the area. "Remember why we're here. Keep your wits about you."

Even cloaked in the opulence of their surroundings, the tension among them was intense, each aware that a single misstep could endanger their mission. The murmur of voices around them was a blend of accents and languages, the sound like a living entity wrapping the quartet in a tapestry of whispered secrets and clandestine transactions.

"Let's split up. We'll cover more ground that way," Jessie suggested, her hazel eyes locking with George's for a moment, communicating a world of meaning in a single glance.

"Indeed," George replied, his words always measured, his demeanour an anchor in the tempest of excitement around them.

"Be careful," Bill added.

"Always am," Jessie said with a half-smile before disappearing into the throng.

As Jessie moved through the crowd, the details of their surroundings imprinted themselves in her mind: the heavy scent of perfume mingling with the mustiness of old money, the way the auctioneer's gavel felt solid and foreboding in her peripheral vision. She knew George, with his methodical thought process, would be cataloguing everything, just as she trusted Isabel's keen observation skills to pick up on the subtleties of human behaviour.

In minutes, they had scattered among the potential buyers, their presence at the illegal auction now woven into the fabric of the night. Each step took them deeper into the heart of darkness they sought to illuminate, their resolve firm beneath the masquerade of their disguises.

"Have you ever seen such a menagerie?" Isabel whispered, her eyes wide as they swept across the room. The venue was alive with the sounds of the exotic: the chittering of a monkey adorned in a tiny waistcoat, the slithering hiss of a snake coiling around a gilded branch, and the restless fluttering of birds with plumage bright enough to shame a rainbow.

"Keep your voice down," Bill hissed back, his gaze darting from one cage to another. "We're not here to gawk."

"Right, collecting evidence," Isabel murmured, pulling out a small notebook and jotting down details.

Jessie sidled closer to a display where the scales of a lizard shimmered like emeralds. Pretending to admire the creature, she snapped a mental picture of the man handling the bids, noting the tattoo peeping from beneath his cuff—a clue worth following up on.

"Wouldn't mind betting that fellow's got more than ink under his sleeve," Jessie muttered to herself, slipping away before her interest became too noticeable.

Meanwhile, George leaned heavily on his cane near a group of potential buyers, their chatter about the next item for bid revealing nothing but greed. He maintained a passive expression while listening intently for any slip-up that might point to the auction's mastermind.

"Quite a specimen, isn't it?" George commented to a portly gentleman ogling an ornate birdcage. "I've heard rumours that these auctions can be... quite exclusive."

"Only the best for those who know where to look," the man replied with a smirk, unwittingly giving George another piece of the puzzle.

Jessie caught George's eye from across the room; her subtle nod was all he needed to know they were getting closer to their quarry. With a shared glance, they reaffirmed their silent pact—they would bring this shady operation to light or die trying.

"Let's hope it doesn't come to that," Jessie thought, heading towards Isabel, who had just uncovered a ledger left carelessly atop a crate. The night was only beginning, and the team were making progress.

A shadow loomed over Jessie as she looked at the ledger Isabel had found. She tensed, feeling the gaze of an unsavoury character sizing her up. The man's eyes, cold and calculating, lingered just a moment too long.

"Looking for something special?" Jessie inquired with feigned innocence, flashing a disarming smile.

"Perhaps," the man grunted, his suspicion obvious. "You don't look like our usual clientele."

"New money," Jessie said smoothly, hoping her charm would defuse the tension. "And new interests."

The man nodded slowly before being swallowed up by the throng of bidders. Jessie let out a silent breath; close calls were part and parcel of undercover work but each one ratcheted up the stakes.

George, meanwhile, exchanged a knowing glance with Bill. They both recognized the tightrope they walked, aware that one misstep could unravel their carefully constructed cover.

"Bill, look lively," George said quietly as he leaned casually against a pillar. "We've attracted some interest."

"Nothing I can't handle," Bill replied with a soft Welsh lilt, his blue eyes vigilant beneath the brim of his fedora.

Just then, Isabel emerged from behind a heavy velvet curtain, her face alight with urgency. "Jessie," she whispered, darting a look around to ensure no ears were prying. "There's more. A hidden room—I caught a glimpse of cages, more animals, some I've never seen before."

"Good work, Isabel," Jessie said, "we need to get those creatures out."

"Agreed," George added. "But we'll need to be sly as foxes. If we're spotted—"

"We won't be," Jessie said in a tone that brooked no argument. "Let's find a way to access that room without drawing attention."

"Time to blend in and make our move," Bill said, adjusting his tie and setting off into the crowd with purpose.

"Stay alert," George cautioned, tapping his cane twice on the ground—a signal they had agreed upon for caution.

The quartet dispersed silently among the attendees, their hearts racing with the knowledge that more than just an auction was at stake. It was a rescue mission now, and every second counted. With quick strides and sharp minds, they navigated through the opulence toward the hidden suffering, ready to confront whatever dangers lay ahead.

STILL INVISIBLE, I WATCHED the team closely and admired the cunning behind Jessie's choice of hand signals—simple, yet effective. A tuck of her auburn strands behind her ear meant 'proceed with caution,' while a seemingly absent-minded scratch at her collar signified 'gather closer.'

"Reminds me of the old alley cat signals," I said to George, who was adjusting his cuffs with calculated nonchalance. "Except less clawing and biting involved."

"Let's hope it stays that way," George replied under his breath, his eyes flickering to Jessie as she subtly signalled for them to converge toward the hidden room's entrance.

"Bill, three o'clock," Jessie whispered, barely moving her lips. "Looks like he's guarding something."

"Got it," Bill responded, tilting his fedora in acknowledgement before casually strolling towards the indicated direction, blending seamlessly with the crowd.

"Isabel, stay behind me," Jessie instructed softly, as Isabel nodded, her eyes keenly observing their surroundings.

"George, you're with me," she continued, her voice a mere breath as they moved through the throng of attendees, their presence as inconspicuous as shadows melding with the dim light.

"Always am," George said with a slight smirk that only Jessie could catch.

"Careful," I said in a low purr, "I sense trouble ahead."

"Your mystical insights or your feline intuition?" George asked, half-teasing.

"Both are never wrong," I said as I probed the room.

I thought the team's communication was seamless, a dance they had perfected over countless encounters and even the newcomer, Isabel, took easily to the game. The air thrummed with tension as they inched closer to the curtain shielding the secret chamber, every nerve alert to the dangers that awaited.

"Wait," Jessie's hand went up, halting their advance. She tilted her head ever so slightly, a signal that caught everyone's attention. They were not alone in their suspicions.

"Someone's watching us," she breathed, just as a figure detached itself from the shadows, its gaze sharp and knowing.

"Trouble indeed," I muttered, as the realisation dawned upon all four that they were no longer unnoticed pawns in this game of deception. Their cover wasn't just blown—it was disintegrated.

"Jessie Harper," the man spoke, stepping forward into the light, revealing features etched with recognition and malice. "And George Jenkins. Your reputation precedes you."

"Can't say the same for you," Jessie replied, her tone cool as ice despite the heat of danger encroaching upon them. "But I guess introductions are now moot."

"Indeed," the man said, a sneer curling his lip. "You've made quite a mess of things, haven't you?"

"Nothing we can't clean up," George said confidently though his mind raced for an exit strategy.

"Is that so?" the man chuckled darkly. "We'll see about that."

The atmosphere crackled with the sudden shift from covert operation to clear and present danger. Jessie and the rest of the team stood united, ready to face whatever came next, their camaraderie their greatest weapon.

"Plan B?" Isabel whispered.

"Plan B," Jessie confirmed.

"Always loved a good 'B,'" I said with a sardonic grin, poised to leap into whatever fray lay ahead.

"Seems like we've got company, and they're not here to bid," Bill muttered under his breath, his gaze darting to the burly men who'd begun to saunter toward our now-exposed quartet. There was a brutish confidence in their stride that spoke louder than any verbal threat.

"Quite the welcoming committee," I quipped, though my mind raced for a way out. The goons had positioned themselves strategically, one at each potential exit. Their eyes, cold and calculating, were locked onto us and I was the only one they could not see.

"Remember the plan," Jessie said, her voice steady as she shifted her stance slightly, ready to move at a moment's notice. "We're not going down without a fight."

"Never thought I'd be tangling with thugs over exotic beasts," I remarked, trying to keep the mood light despite the gravity of our situation. "Next time, let's stick to haunted houses, shall we?"

"Focus, Khan," George reprimanded gently, though the ghost of a smile flickered across his face. His cane was now held more like a weapon than a support.

"Right, then." Isabel clutched her purse tighter, an innocent accessory that I knew housed more than just lipstick and powder. "When I say 'now,' we make our move." Isabel added.

"Looking for these?" one of the gang members sneered, holding up a set of keys triumphantly. "Thought you might be sneaking off with our prized possessions. Not on your Nellie."

"Those wouldn't happen to be the keys to your heart, would they?" Jessie asked, earning a glare that could curdle milk. "No? Worth a shot."

"Now!" Isabel shouted.

Chairs toppled as the quartet sprang into action, using them as barriers between them and the advancing thugs. Jessie swung her leg up, kicking a tray of drinks into one man's path, sending him slipping and sliding in an undignified dance.

"Sorry about the mess," she called out, not sounding sorry at all.

"Khan, left side!" George yelled, and I leapt to intercept a hulking figure trying to flank us. As I tripped him, my paws swiped a heavy silver candlestick—probably worth a pretty penny—into the path of Bill who picked it up using it as a club.

"Take that, you ruffian!" Bill said as he swung again.

"Nice swing," I said having just watched Bill dispatch another with a swift right hook. "Boxing lessons paying off, I see."

"Always be prepared," I grinned, ducking as an ashtray flew over my head. "Scouts' honour."

"Can we save the banter for after we escape?" Jessie chided, even as she deftly avoided a lunging grab, her tailored suit allowing for impressive flexibility. "George, behind you!"

"Got it," George responded, his cane sweeping out in a calculated arc, striking the shins of an assailant who howled in pain.

"Like swatting flies," Isabel commented dryly, her purse proving to be more versatile than expected when she smacked a thug square in the jaw with it.

"Tell me there's a brick in there," I said, impressed.

"Better still. A first edition of Agatha Christie," she replied with a smirk.

"Blimey, those are lethal," Bill said, almost admiringly.

"Everyone accounted for?" Jessie checked quickly as we regrouped, ready for the next wave.

"Present and still on active duty," I said swishing my tail.

"Let's keep it that way... for all of us ... visible and otherwise," George said, his dark eyes on the alert for the next threat. "Stick together and remember why we're here."

"Justice, saving exotic creatures, and because we can't resist a good mystery?" I offered.

"Exactly, but let us concentrate on these ruffians," Jessie said with fire in her soul. "Now let's get out of this alive so we can actually solve it."

I weaved my way through the chaos on silent paws. Jessie launched herself over a toppled cage, catching a gang member by surprise. Her fist connected with his jaw, and she pivoted, sweeping her leg to knock another off balance.

"Nice move!" I called out but I don't think anyone heard me above the din. I was getting concerned we were losing ground so I shifted into an imposing black panther, causing a would-be attacker to stumble backward in shock.

"Intimidation: always effective," I purred and amazed I could still find amusement even amidst the fracas.

"Can we focus, please?" George's cane was a blur, each strike precise and effective, creating a barrier between us and our assailants.

"Right behind you," Bill grunted, locking arms with a thug twice his size and judo-flipping him onto a pile of crates.

"Never knew auctions could be so... physical," Isabel remarked, her eyes darting around for the next threat.

"Stick with us, love; it's never dull," I said, shifting back to cat form and leaping onto an aggressor's shoulders, claws outstretched.

"Khan! A little warning next time?" Jessie admonished, though I could tell she was grateful as the man flailed, trying to dislodge me.

"Where's the fun in that?" I said, jumping down as he crumpled to the ground.

"Everyone still with me?" George's voice cut through the cacophony, his gaze steady as he surveyed our ragtag group.

"Still here," Jessie confirmed, pushing a stray lock of hair from her face. "Isabel?"

"Present, and rather enjoying this," she replied, swinging her purse like a medieval flail.

"Bill?"

"Wouldn't miss it," Bill said, dusting off his hands after dispatching another foe.

"Khan?"

"Nine lives and counting," I joked. "Now, let's find those creatures."

"Over there," Isabel pointed to the heavy curtain veiling a hidden area. "That's where they're keeping them."

"Then that's where we're going," George said.

"Let's make it quick," I suggested. "I have a dinner date with a can of tuna that I'd hate to postpone."

"Always about your stomach," Jessie teased, but her smile was fleeting as we approached the curtain.

"Ready?" George asked as he watched for our reaction.

"Ready," we echoed, a chorus of determination.

With a swift movement, George pulled the curtain aside, revealing cages filled with exotic, frightened creatures. Their plaintive cries tugged at my feline heartstrings.

"Time to end this," Jessie said.

"Correct," I said, ready to leap into action. "After all, we're not just investigators; we're rescuers too."

"Right," George nodded, and together we advanced toward the caged animals ready to dismantle the operation and protect the innocent.

"George, left side!" Jessie's voice cut through the cacophony of growls and hisses emanating from the cages. Her eyes were fixed on a pair of bulky men rushing towards us, their intentions clear by the clubs in their hands.

"Already on it," George replied, swinging his cane with an elegance that belied its deadly intention. The first assailant stumbled back, caught off-guard by the precision of the blow.

"Isabel, duck!" I warned as a burly figure lunged towards her from behind. She dropped to the ground with grace, tripping the attacker with a swift leg sweep.

"Thanks, Khan! I owe you one," she panted, scrambling to her feet just as another adversary dove at her.

"Keep the IOU chitties running," I quipped, my claws unsheathed and ready for action.

"Khan, above you!" Jessie shouted.

I looked up just in time to see a shadow descending from the rafters. Twisting agilely, I darted away as a net crashed down where I had stood moments before.

"Nice try, but you'll have to be quicker than that," I said with a smirk, eyeing the frustrated henchman now entangled in his own trap.

"We don't have much time," Jessie urged, her gaze flickering between us and the creatures. "We need to get these animals out of here."

"Yes," George said adjusting his grip on his cane. "But first, we have to deal with this lot."

"Leave it to me," Bill said, picking up a nearby chair and wielding it like a shield. He charged forward, forcing the encroaching gang members into retreat with each forward step.

"Resourceful, isn't he?" I observed dryly.

"Comes with the territory," Jessie replied, her attention never wavering from the task at hand.

"Look out!" George's warning came just in time for me to evade a wayward kick that would have sent a lesser feline sprawling.

"Clumsy oaf," I sneered at the thug who missed me. "You fight like a blind dog chasing its tail."

"Khan, always the charmer," Jessie chortled, dispatching another foe with a swift jab.

"Charisma is part of the package, dear Jessie," I replied, leaping onto a cage and launching myself at the next wave of attackers.

"Focus! We're not out yet," George reminded us, his calm voice grounding amidst the chaos.

"Right," Jessie agreed, breathing heavily. "Let's find a way out."

"Over there!" Isabel pointed to a door half-hidden behind a stack of crates.

"Move!" George commanded, and we made a break for it.

"Almost there," I thought, sensing freedom and the company of alley cats just beyond the threshold.

Just as we reached the door, an ominous click resonated through the air, freezing us in our tracks. We turned to see the barrel of a gun aimed directly at us, held by none other than the auctioneer himself.

"Thought you could outsmart me, did you?" he sneered.

"Put the gun down," Jessie commanded, her voice steady despite the danger.

"Sorry, sweetheart. This game ends now," he replied with a malicious grin.

"Khan, any ideas?" George whispered, eyeing the weapon warily.

"Working on it," I murmured, but even my quick wit was struggling against the stark reality of cold steel.

"Last chance," the auctioneer taunted, his finger twitching on the trigger.

"Jessie, George, look out!" I cried as the world seemed to slow down, the auctioneer's face contorting with triumph.

Jessie heard a gunshot echoing in the enclosed space.

Chapter Twelve

THE BITING GAG IN Jessie's mouth tasted like dust and despair. She wriggled in her chair, the ropes biting into her wrists with every twist. The warehouse was a dark maze, each room a carbon copy of gloom. She heard muffled grunts from what she assumed were George, Bill, and Isabel in their own quarters of captivity. At the thought of those three, she recalled the gunshot and hoped Khan was alright.

"Right then," she muttered through the gag, her voice a muffled growl of determination. "This is no time for a damsel-in-distress act."

With the pragmatism of a woman who's had her fair share of tight spots, Jessie shuffled her chair, inch by painstaking inch, towards the nearest wall. Her hazel eyes accented by the smattering of freckles across her nose, darted around the dimly lit space. It was a shabby excuse for a prison; the captors clearly amateurs in the art of confinement.

"Whoever tied these knots must've been a boy scout dropout," she thought, humour finding its way even in dire circumstances, much like Khan would have appreciated.

She leaned against the wall, feeling for any irregularity, anything that might be fashioned into a tool. Her fingers brushed over the rough texture of bricks until they met something colder, harder—metal. A loose screw protruded just enough for her to work it against the rope.

"Ha!" she thought and her spirits lifted, "Who needs pick-locks when you've got poor craftsmanship on your side?"

Jessie worked tirelessly, sawing the rope against the screw's thread. The bonds loosened, giving way to hope and a slight burn on her skin—a small price for freedom.

"Almost there," she encouraged herself, her internal monologue taking on the role of a touchline supporter.

Finally, the last strand snapped. Jessie flung off the remnants of the rope, pulling the gag away and rubbing her sore wrists. She stood up, stretching her legs, now free to explore the rest of the warehouse and regroup with the others.

"Time to show these clowns the door," Jessie said with a wry smile, simulating Khan's bravado as she prepared to tackle the next obstacle. Jessie Harper was not one to fold when things got interesting.

In another room, George wriggled his toes taking stock of the situation. His usual dry humour lodged in his throat behind the gag. Stuck in a room that felt more like a coffin than an architect's blunder, he had to admit, this wasn't how he envisioned spending his evening.

"Think, Jenkins," he muttered against the fabric stifling his words. His bound hands fumbled across the floorboards, sensing each joint and nail. He pressed down, feeling for give or creaks, any sign of a hidden compartment or exit.

"Ah, what do we have here?" A smirk played on his lips as he discovered one board with more play than the others. Easing his fingers beneath it, he jimmied it up just enough to reveal a glint of metal. A pick-lock! He almost laughed at the irony — the captors' oversight was their downfall. With painstaking precision, he worked the locks with his bound wrists, tension coiling within him until the click of the lock resounded like victory.

"Should've known better than to try and cage an old war dog like me," George whispered triumphantly, shaking off the ropes and removing his gag. If only there were an audience to appreciate his escape artistry.

Meanwhile, Bill Roberts' ears were his best asset now. Straining against the silence, he caught the murmur of voices. It took every ounce of his detective-trained restraint not to shout for attention. Instead, he listened, head cocked, deciphering the muffled words slipping through the cracks.

"Creatures... tonight... shipment..." The snatches of conversation outside were breadcrumbs leading to the loaf — in this case, the bigger picture of their captors' plan. Roberts committed each word to memory, a mental note taken with the precision of Morse code.

"Cheeky buggers," he thought, his Welsh tenor echoing inside his head. "So, you're smugglers and kidnappers, then? Two crimes for the price of one."

He could imagine Khan's quip if he were here, something about a 'buy one, get one free' deal gone awry. A corner of Bill's mouth twitched in reluctant amusement. Humour in dire straits was a coping mechanism, after all, and it seemed even thoughts of Khan could invoke it.

The scene set, both men worked in their respective confines, their collective goal singular — to reunite with Jessie and Isabel and thwart the plans of those who dared cross the Dale Street Private Investigations Agency. Each twist of the pick-lock, each deciphered whisper, brought them closer to turning the tables on their captors. And when they did, George Jenkins and Bill Roberts would ensure it was done with the cunning of detectives and the flourish of a great escape.

Isabel's breath came in short, shallow gasps, the sound loud in the confines of her dimly lit prison. Her hands were bound tightly behind her back, the coarse rope biting into her delicate wrists. She shifted her weight on the cold concrete floor, trying to ignore the fear gnawing at her insides.

"Come now, Isabel," she whispered. "You've read about worse predicaments in those dusty old tomes at the office." She closed her eyes, summoning images of the creatures she had catalogued just weeks prior in a rare paranormal compendium.

"Griffins," she began tentatively, speaking as if lecturing an unseen audience, "proud and noble, with the keen sight of an eagle and the strength of a lion. Oh, how I could use their wings to fly out of this fix."

Her mind danced from creature to creature, seeking solace in the knowledge that she, too, possessed qualities akin to those mythical beings. "And then there are the selkies, slipping free from their binds with the ease of shedding a skin..." Isabel's voice trailed off as resolve kindled within her.

"Right," she resolved, her tone firmer now. "Slip free. Outsmart them. If a selkie can do it, so can I."

JESSIE STOOD UP QUIETLY, rubbing her sore wrists. There was no time to waste; George and Bill were counting on her. It was time to gather the team, rescue the exotic creatures, and put an end to this shady operation. And maybe, just maybe, she'd let George take her out for that celebratory glass of champagne he'd been hinting at—if they made it out alive.

Bill was still listening as his mind was putting the pieces together. Exotic creatures, likely the ones they'd been investigating, and they were in immediate danger. He needed to act, and fast. With a degree of urgency, he wriggled against his confines, silently promising those creatures—and himself—that he wouldn't let them down.

"Once I'm out of here, it's going to take more than a couple of crooks to stop me," Bill thought determinedly. He pictured George's methodical approach blending with Jessie's resourcefulness, and despite the gravity of their situation, a faint smile tugged at the corners of his mouth.

"Teamwork is the key. We'll show these thugs the door... preferably with a swift kick to their backsides."

"Ah, the past does come in handy," Isabel muttered to herself, managing to use her fingers behind her back to trace the familiar groove in the wall. During the scuffle with their captors, she'd been shoved against this very panel, and it had given way slightly under her weight. A hidden door—how quaint, she thought wryly.

She pressed firmly, and with a faint click, the panel swung open, revealing a narrow passage suffused with dim light. Isabel peered through, her heart pounding. This was it; the room where they held the creatures must be on the other side.

"Spooky corridors, secret rooms—just another day at the office," she chuckled, easing into the passage. The walls were close, the air stale, but Isabel moved with purpose, guided by the sliver of hope that they could still turn this around.

Emerging into the adjoining room, Isabel gasped. Cages lined the walls, each containing a creature more wondrous and bizarre than the last. Their eyes glowed in the dimness, intelligent and frightened. She'd read about these beings in dusty tomes, never imagining she'd see them in the flesh.

"Right, you lot," Isabel said, though the gag made her words muffled. "Time for a jailbreak."

HAVING FREED THEMSELVES OF their bonds, Jessie and George made their way slowly through the maze until

Jessie heard muffled words that sounded like Isabel and some strange animal sounds.

"Isabel!" Jessie's voice cut through the shadows as she, George, and Bill converged in the creature-filled room. "You found them!"

"Yes, but can you untie my hands first," Isabel said as she turned around displaying her hands bound behind her back.

"Indeed," George replied, his cane tapping the floor as he surveyed the cages and watched Jessie free Isabel's hands. "Now, to liberate these poor souls."

"An impeccable timing for an uninvited guest," I said as the mastermind strode into the room. My fur bristled and I sensed the tension in the room coil like a spring about to snap.

"Ah, the infamous trio from Dale Street and their talking cat," sneered the figure before them, removing the hooded cape that had shrouded their identity. "You've meddled in my affairs for the last time."

George adjusted his grip on his cane, eyes sharp beneath the shadow of his homburg hat. "I must say, your disguise was almost as good as your intentions were bad."

"Almost?" Jessie stepped forward, her stance as unyielding as her tone. "We've unravelled your little tapestry of crime, and it ends here."

"Unravelled? How quaint." The mastermind's laugh was cold, devoid of mirth. "You think you have me cornered, but—"

"Cornered, captured, cuffed," Bill interrupted, lunging forward with surprising agility. He twisted the culprit's arm behind their back, pressing them against the nearest cage. "You'll find my police training isn't easily outsmarted. Edward Kingsley, you are under arrest."

"Ooh, that's got to sting more than a nettle tea bath," I chuckled, my tail swishing with satisfaction.

"Bill, remind me to never get on your bad side," George said, a smirk playing on his lips as he watched their former adversary now secured by handcuffs.

"Right then," Jessie clapped her hands together, her gaze sweeping across the dimly lit facility. "Time to shine a light on this operation. Let's gather evidence before the authorities arrive."

"Photographs first," George suggested as he retrieved his pocket camera from inside his jacket. "We'll need these for the records."

"Records, schmecords," I said with a dismissive flick of my paw. "I say we go for the dramatic reveal. Imagine the headlines!"

"Khan, sometimes I wonder if you're more interested in theatrics than justice," Jessie teased, rifling through papers on a nearby desk. "Aha, shipping manifests and transaction logs. These should prove quite enlightening."

"Enlightening and incriminating," Bill added as George snapped pictures of the cages and the documents spread out before them.

"Nothing says guilty quite like a paper trail," George said. "It's the breadcrumbs that lead us to the gingerbread house."

"Except our witch is already in the candy oven," I said, hopping onto the desk to survey the scene. "And I do love a good fairy tale ending."

"Let's not count our chickens just yet," Jessie cautioned, her expression softening as she glanced at George. "We still have work to do."

"Work, schmerk," Khan said playfully. "With the mastermind in cuffs and their secrets laid bare, I'd say this is another case closed for the Dale Street Private Investigations Agency."

"Indeed," George concurred. "And once again, it's our combined efforts that brought down the curtain on this sordid affair."

"Combined efforts and a touch of feline charm," I added with a wink. "After all, what's a mystery without a little magic?"

"Or a lot of magic, in your case," Jessie laughed, her eyes glinting with mirth. "Now, let's wrap this up. We've got a lot of paperwork ahead."

"Paperwork, schmaperwork," I sighed dramatically but even I couldn't hide the pride in my voice. "All in a day's work for paranormal investigators extraordinaire."

As we continued to document the evidence around us, our camaraderie never wavered, each member of the team acutely aware that our strength lay not just in our individual skills, but in the unbreakable bond we shared. And as the laughter and banter filled the room, so too did the unmistakable sense of triumph over darkness.

"Right, you lot, stand back," I said with a flourish of my tail. My green eyes shimmered in the dim light of the room as I prepared my spell. "Time to send our SOS." I moved my paws in an intricate pattern and an ethereal glow enveloped my whiskers.

"Is it working?" Jessie peered over my furry shoulder, her curiosity piqued.

"Patience, Harper. Magical messaging is an art, not a parlour trick," I chided without breaking concentration. With a final flick of my paw, the glow shot upwards, piercing the industrial ceiling and vanishing into the ether.

"Blimey," Bill muttered, impressed despite himself.

"Authorities alerted. I do love it when things go according to plan," George said, tipping his homburg hat back with a relieved smile.

"According to plan? You make it sound as if we expected to be in a secret warehouse filled with contraband creatures today," Jessie joked as her freckles danced as she grinned.

"Ah, but the best plans are the ones that allow for... improvisation," George countered, his cane tapping rhythmically on the concrete floor.

"Speaking of which," Jessie started, her gaze turning towards the cages, "we need to get these poor souls out of here."

"Allow me to offer my expertise," George said as he approached the first cage, lock-picking tools at the ready. "Bill, keep watch at the door. Jessie, help me with the locks?"

"Of course," she said, moving to assist.

"Meanwhile, I'll do what I do best—provide moral support and devastatingly good looks," I added, eliciting chuckles from my companions.

As George worked on the locks with Jessie, Isabel and Bill standing by, ready to open the cages, the atmosphere amongst us was one of focus mixed with a touch of levity—a testament to our shared experiences and the bond we had formed.

"Almost... there," George murmured, and with a satisfying click, the lock turned. The cage door swung open, revealing a pair of shivering exotic creatures.

"Freedom awaits, exotic ones," I said in a calm, measured tone. They responded with a soft mew almost like a cat as their bodies relaxed sensing the sincerity in my voice.

The remainder of the cages were opened and the creatures of all shapes and sizes were released.

"Alright, let's move them all out. Carefully now," Jessie instructed, gently ushering the creatures into transport carriers they had arranged.

"Next stop: Regents Park Zoo," I said knowing that they would be safe there and I watched with satisfaction as each creature was secured for the journey. "A much-deserved retreat after this harrowing ordeal, wouldn't you say?"

"Indeed," George agreed, closing another carrier door with care. "These creatures deserve peace and safety."

"Safe and sound, thanks to us," Bill said, returning from his lookout post. "The cavalry should be arriving any minute now, thanks to our magical feline friend, and we can hand over Edward Kingsley to the police."

"Ah, think nothing of it," I replied with feigned humility. "But remember, it's Khan the Magnificent when you tell this tale."

"Khan the Magnificent," Jessie echoed, shaking her head with a fond smile. "We'll make sure your heroics are duly noted."

"Heroics, schmeroics," I flicked my tail dismissively. "Let's just say I'm purring with contentment at a job well done."

"Contentment? I thought that was indigestion from the sardine sandwich you snatched earlier," George teased.

"Ha! Shows what you know. My stomach is a temple," I retorted and the group erupted into laughter as they completed their rescue mission, bantering all the while amidst the echoes of unlocking cages and the soft coos and growls of grateful creatures.

With the last of the animals safely stowed away and the police Black Maria had carted Kingsley off to jail, I, together with Jessie, George, Bill Roberts and Isabel made our way out of the building. As we stepped into the Clerkenwell night, the air was thick with anticipation of justice served and adventures yet to come.

The Dale Street Private Investigations Agency seemed like it was a million miles away as we navigated the fog-kissed streets of London. The night's events lay heavy on our shoulders, though not as heavy as the burden of injustice that had driven us into the shadows of peril in the first place.

"Remind me again why we couldn't have brought at least one of those flying critters?" I said as I weaved between the team's legs with an agility that belied the night's earlier tribulations. "Would've made for a quicker journey back."

"Because that would have been conspicuous, and you know it," Jessie retorted, her breath forming clouds in the chill air. "Besides, I think we've had enough excitement for one evening, don't you?"

"Excitement is one word for it," George added, the corners of his mouth twitching upwards. "Though I'm rather fond of 'near-death experience' myself."

"Ah, but what is life without a brush with mortality to remind us of our purpose?" I said, eliciting a laugh from Isabel who trailed slightly behind, her arms wrapped around herself as if to ward off more than just the cold.

"Your philosophical musings aside," Bill said, "we did well tonight. Some of those creatures are safe because of us."

"Safe and likely plotting their next mischief," George said, his voice tinged with a warmth that only a shared ordeal can forge. "But indeed, well done everyone."

"Speaking of plotting," Jessie said, her gaze fixed on the road ahead, "our next step is bringing down those responsible. We can't allow them to continue exploiting these creatures for their gain."

"Never fear, Jessie," I said, bounding up onto a wall to survey their progress. "With my strategic prowess and your tenacious sleuthing, they don't stand a chance."

"Modesty isn't your strong suit, is it?" Isabel chuckled, shaking her head but unable to hide her affection for the unfathomable cat.

"Modesty doesn't solve mysteries, my dear Isabel," I replied, leaping down to rejoin the group. "But fear not, I shall leave some of the glory for the rest of you."

"Generous of you," George remarked dryly, the hint of a smile still playing on his lips.

"Indeed," Jessie agreed, her tone light despite the gravity of their conversation. "Now, let's get off the street and warm up. We've got plans to make and a gang to bring to justice."

"Lead on, fearless leader," I said, giving Jessie a mock bow, my green eyes gleaming with the promise of adventure. "I do believe there's a pot of tea with our names on it."

"Finally, something we can all agree on," Bill said, his voice filled with relief as we approached the welcoming lights of Mrs Swarbrick's lodging house, a sanctuary amidst the chaos of an uncertain world.

Chapter Thirteen

"Ah, the sweet scent of victory—and is that a hint of Earl Grey?" I said as I sauntered into the lodging house's cozy kitchen. My green eyes gleamed with satisfaction as I hopped onto the counter, watching Jessie pour steaming water into a teapot.

"Victory indeed," Jessie replied, her auburn hair now cascading freely around her shoulders. "I can hardly believe we managed to pull it off without a hitch."

"Without a hitch? I'd call George's lock-picking extravaganza more than just a 'hitch,'" Bill Roberts chuckled, settling into one of the mismatched chairs at the kitchen table.

"Extravaganza is an overstatement," George said leaning on his cane with a self-deprecating smile. "But it did the trick."

"More than just a trick, my dear George," I said curling my tail around myself. "You wield those tools like an artist."

"Here's to artists and magicians alike," Jessie raised her cup, the steam curling up toward her freckled cheeks.

"Cheers," they all echoed, clinking cups and mugs in the heart of their sanctuary, the buzz of success warming them more than any tea could.

"Speaking of magicians," George said eyeing the black cat, "the word on the paranormal street is that Khan the Magnificent's antics have been quite the sensation."

"Word travels fast in our circles," Jessie added, her eyes twinkling with amusement. "It appears our feline friend here has become something of a legend."

"Legend, you say? Well, I suppose I can live with that title," I replied feigning indifference whilst my eyes betrayed a glint of pride.

"Your humility knows no bounds, Khan," Bill said with a laugh.

"Of course, it's not just Khan receiving accolades," George pointed out. "The entire team has been commended for bravery and dedication to justice."

"Commendations are well and good," Jessie admitted, "but seeing those creatures safe—that's the real reward."

"Indeed. And let's not forget, this case might put us one step closer to becoming England's foremost private investigators," George added, stroking his moustache thoughtfully.

"Foremost or not, we're a heck of a team," Bill stated firmly. "And I'd say that calls for another round of tea—or something stronger."

"Tea will suffice for now," Jessie said, standing up to refill the pot. "We've got plenty of time for stronger celebrations later."

"Agreed," George replied, the corners of his mouth lifting ever so slightly. "For now, let's enjoy the quiet after the storm."

"Quiet? With this lot?" I said eliciting another round of laughter from the group. "I'd wager the quiet won't last long—not with the adventures that await the Dale Street Private Investigations Agency."

"Adventures that we'll face together," Jessie affirmed, her gaze meeting each of hers companions in turn.

"Wouldn't have it any other way," Bill agreed.

"Nor would I," George concurred.

"Does this include me?" Isabel said.

"Of course!" Jessie said.

"Then it's settled," I said, my voice smooth as silk. "To future escapades and the enduring camaraderie of this exceptional agency."

"Hear, hear!" they all chorused, raising their cups once more, the warmth of the room encapsulating the essence of their bond—a team united in purpose and unfaltering friendship.

I stretched languidly across the kitchen windowsill looking down at the room with casual indifference. Below me, the human quartet of Jessie, George, Isabel and Bill stood in the aftermath of triumph, a shared silence stretching between them like the last note of a symphony hanging in the air.

"Marvellous job today, wasn't it?" I purred, breaking the stillness. "Rescued the creatures, nabbed the villain—quite the thrilling chapter for our little enterprise."

Jessie's gaze flicked toward George, then back to me. "Yes, Khan, it was quite the day," she replied, her voice steady but tinged with something unspoken.

"Indeed." George's cane tapped against the wooden floor as he edged closer to Jessie. "Although, some might say the real adventure lies not in the chase, but in what comes after."

"Profound," I remarked with a lazy swish of my tail. "Did you find that gem in a fortune cookie, or is it original Jenkins wisdom?"

George chuckled, the sound rumbling from deep within his chest. "Just an observation, Khan. But speaking of observations, Jessie, there's something I've been meaning to discuss with you."

"Is that so?" Jessie tilted her head, the softening of her expression noticeable even to a feline such as me.

"Quite so," George confirmed. "We've been through a great deal together, faced dangers most would flinch at. And through it all, we have grown... close. Closer than I ever anticipated when we started this agency."

"George..." Jessie took a half step forward, her freckled cheeks warming with a blush that complimented her auburn hair. "I feel the same. We make an excellent team, professionally. But I think... I think it's time we explore where these feelings could lead us personally."

"Ah, romance!" I interjected, leaping down from my perch to twine around their ankles. "A classic tale: detective meets detective, they solve crimes, fall in love, and live happily ever after. Or until the next case pops up."

"Khan, do you ever take anything seriously?" Jessie asked, though a smile played at her lips.

"Only the serious business of being charming and dashing," I said. "And speaking of which, let me regale you with a tale of my own."

"Please do," George said, his arm finding its way around Jessie's waist as they turned their attention to me. "Your stories are always... enlightening."

"Delighted to entertain," I began, pacing before all the team with a theatrical flair. "You see, during one of my midnight escapades across the rooftops of Liverpool, I encountered a rather pompous pigeon. This bird had the audacity to claim he was the fastest creature on wings or paws. Naturally, I couldn't let such a statement stand uncontested."

"Of course not," Jessie said, her laughter mingling with George's.

"So, I challenged him to a race," I continued. "From the Royal Liver Building to the docks. The entire time, that bird squawked about his inevitable victory, but as we neared the finish line, I may have accidentally sent a cluster of startled seagulls into his path. Chaos ensued, feathers flew, and who should emerge victorious but yours truly."

"Accidentally, you say?" George raised an eyebrow.

"Purely accidental," I affirmed with a sly wink. "But let that be a lesson: Never underestimate a cat, especially one with my cunning and speed."

"Or your modesty," Jessie teased.

"Modesty is for those with less to boast about," I shot back with pride.

"Indeed," George agreed, the warmth in his tone mirroring the fond look he shared with Jessie. "But let's not discount the value of teamwork. After all, it's what has brought us to this moment."

"Teamwork and a touch of magic," Jessie added, her gaze locked with George's. "Something tells me we're just getting started."

"Here's to getting started then," I declared, raising an imaginary glass. "To Jessie and George, may your partnership thrive both in work and in matters of the heart. And to Isabel, our best new member and not forgetting Bill, of course, our worthy mentor."

"Cheers to that," they said in unison, their eyes reflecting the promise of new beginnings.

As George and Jessie leaned in for a tentative yet tender kiss, I decided to leave the humans to their moment, bounding off to find a quiet corner to nap. After all, even enigmatic felines need their beauty rest.

Chapter Fourteen

THE NEXT DAY

"Cheers!" The word resounded through Bill's makeshift office at Scotland Yard, a chorus of crystal clinking against crystal. I, Khan, being of feline persuasion and rather disinclined to partake in human libations, watched from atop a filing cabinet as my associates continued to celebrate our recent triumph.

"Here's to us," Jessie said with her eyes sparkling with pride as she raised her glass higher. "To teamwork and tenacity!"

"May we continue to outwit scoundrels and scallywags," George added with his characteristic dry wit, his moustache twitching slightly above a smile.

"Especially those with an unhealthy interest in our four-legged friends," Bill chimed in, his Welsh accent turning the words into a melodic toast.

"Couldn't have done it without each one of you," Jessie said, directing a nod towards Isabel who beamed back, her hands clasped around her own glass.

"Or me," I interjected with a purr that rippled through the room, earning chuckles and a round of nods.

"Indeed, Khan," Jessie agreed, glancing up at me with a smirk. "Your... unique insights proved invaluable."

"Unique is one way to put it," George remarked, amusement flickering in his dark eyes.

"Speaking of our four-legged clients," Jessie began, setting down her glass with a decisive click on the desk. "I think it'd be a splendid idea for us to personally visit each of the stolen cats' owners. It would show our commitment and give those poor creatures a proper send-off."

"Brilliant, and possibly the millionaire with the private zoo in Surrey who owned the stolen exotic creatures," Isabel said, clapping her hands softly. "They've been through so much; they deserve a heartwarming reunion."

"Yes, you're right, Isabel, plus, it will give us a chance to ensure no lingering threads from the case remain untied," George added, ever the meticulous investigator.

"There are other loose ends other than visiting the owners of the rescued cats and creatures," Jessie said, "but we will get around to that after we have seen the owners."

"First stop, Lady Pandora Street-Walters and her Mr Whiskers," Bill said pulling out his pocket notebook and flipping through the pages.

My tail swished thoughtfully. "Does she still keep that obnoxious parrot? Last time I visited, the bird had the audacity to call me 'whisker face.'"

Laughter filled the room, and Jessie shook her head, chuckling. "Only you, Khan, could start a feud with a parrot."

"Feud?" I lifted my chin with feline dignity. "I merely refuse to engage in conversation with lesser creatures."

"Right," George said, grinning. "We'll make sure to keep the two of you apart."

"Let's map out our route," Jessie suggested, pulling a Greater London atlas closer. The team huddled together, planning the visits with military precision—a strategy not unlike preparing for battle, though this time armed with kindness rather than cunning.

"Alright, team," Jessie concluded, snapping the atlas shut. "Let's give these cats the homecoming they deserve."

"Indeed," I purred from my vantage point. "After all, what's life without a touch of grace and gratitude?"

"Spoken like a true gentleman," Isabel teased, and I couldn't help but preen under the praise.

"Shall we depart then?" George asked, reaching for his cane and hat.

"Lead the way," Bill responded, tipping his head towards the door.

"Adventure awaits," Jessie said with a determined glint in her eye, and together, they set off to congratulate the owners on being reunited with their pedigree cats.

"Adventure," I whispered to myself, leaping down from the cabinet. "And perhaps a bit of salmon, if I play my cards right."

I INVISIBLY SAUNTERED THROUGH the marble-floored foyer of Lady Pandora Street-Walters' Mayfair house, my tail held high with an air of self-importance that belied my recent harrowing escapades. The opulence of the place was not lost on me—gilded mirrors, plush velvet settees, and a crystal chandelier that sparkled in the sunlight streaming through the tall windows.

"Ah, Your Ladyship," Jessie greeted as our hostess emerged from the depths of her grand residence, the very picture of old-world grace save for the tears glistening in her eyes.

"Miss Harper, Mr Jenkins, Sergeant Roberts and everyone, I cannot express my gratitude," Lady Pandora exclaimed, her voice quivering with emotion. "My dear Mr Whiskers—he means the world to me."

"Seeing our furry friends back where they belong is all the thanks we need," George replied, his eyes warm with the satisfaction of a job well done. He leaned slightly on his cane, standing beside Jessie like a steadfast guardian of justice.

"Your Ladyship, this is Isabel. The newest member of our investigative team," Jessie said.

"Please, Pandora will suffice," Lady Pandora said, "and Isabel, it's good to meet you."

"Would it be too much to ask to see Mr Whiskers?" Isabel inquired, her tone gentle to match the moment.

"Of course not, my dear, come right this way." Lady Pandora led us into a sunlit parlour where the returned Persian cat sat atop a satin cushion like royalty awaiting its subjects.

"Mr Whiskers!" Lady Pandora cried out, sweeping the fluffy feline into her arms. The cat, unperturbed by the sudden display of affection, simply purred and nuzzled against her.

"Is there anything more pure than the love between a cat and their human?" I said telepathically so only Jessie could hear, unable to resist the tenderness of the scene.

"Thank you, Your Ladyship," Bill said ignoring the invitation to informality, "we really must leave as we have several owners to see."

"Lady Penelope Worthington's Mayfair townhouse and her prize Persian," George said, consulting the list in his hand.

"Shall we then?" Jessie asked, and we nodded in agreement, leaving Lady Pandora with her precious Mr Whiskers and stepping out into the crisp London air.

As we piled into the borrowed police car, Bill behind the wheel, I couldn't help but remark, "Do you suppose Lady Penelope's Persian will be as amenable to a heartfelt embrace?"

"Knowing Sir Percy Worthington, the General, he's trained the cat to salute him," George chuckled, prompting laughter from the group.

"Let's hope our next reunion is less military and more merriment," Jessie said, her eyes catching George's for a fleeting moment that spoke volumes.

"Off to the Worthington's then," Isabel declared, and with a turn of the key, Bill set off driving sedately through Mayfair streets.

It was very much the same scenario at the home of Lady Worthington as it had been at Lady Pandora's home. The same could be said for the next two on the list: Lord and Lady Featherstone and their Siamese and at the luxury Westminster flat of Mrs Langford and her pedigree cat, Duchess.

The team found it satisfying to see owners and cats so happy but were anxious to progress in clearing up all the loose ends. Bill must have been reading the team's collective mindset as he said, "I suggest we have a trip out into the country before we do some work on tying up the loose ends of the investigation."

Bill relaxed at the wheel on leaving the city behind for the rolling green hills of Surrey.

"Adventure and sentiment," I thought, watching the landscape blur past. "Today is a fine day for both."

On reaching our destination, the gravel crunched beneath our feet as we approached the grand façade of the country estate belonging to the American millionaire, Martin Rothschild. A stern-faced butler, whose posture rivalled that of a royal guard, welcomed us at the door with a curt nod and ushered us through to the study.

"Mr Rothschild will see you presently," he announced in a voice that brooked no argument, then retreated, leaving us in the company of dark oak panels and the scent of leather-bound books.

"Feels like we've stepped into a military stronghold rather than a home," George whispered, eyeing the numerous medals and commendations adorning the walls.

Before Jessie could respond, the door swung open and in strode the millionaire, his presence filling the room like a gust from the hills. His eyes, however, softened upon seeing the Siamese cat cradled in Bill's arms.

"Ah, there you are, my brave little soldier!" he said extending his arms for his feline companion.

The cat leaped into the Rothschild's embrace and the stern mask fell away to reveal a man overjoyed at the return of his comrade-in-arms. The millionaire's grizzled face broke into a rare smile as he nuzzled the Siamese, who purred contentedly.

"Never thought I'd see a general undone by a bundle of fur," I thought, my invisible tail flicking with amusement. "A strategic weakness, perhaps?"

The Siamese cat looked at me so I put a paw to my mouth in a shushing gesture. The Siamese grinned realising he was the only one who could see me.

"So, you are the people responsible for returning my collection?" Rothschild thundered.

"We are, and please permit me to introduce everyone," Bill said. "This is Jessie Harper and her business partner, George Jenkins, and their able associate Isabel Kershaw. I'm Detective Sergeant Bill Roberts."

"From the Metropolitan Police, I assume," Rothschild said.

"No, sir, from the Liverpool City Police on secondment."

"That makes sense. The Commissioner telephoned and admitted there had been some police corruption involved in both criminal operations."

"Sad to say, but that is correct, sir," Bill said.

"Do you mind if I ask a question?" Isabel said.

"Not at all, Miss Kershaw, what do you wish to know?"

"Why do you collect exotic creatures?" Isabel said.

"I'm a collector of the unusual and a collector of artefacts that I'm interested in," Rothschild said without the slightest hint that he had been offended by Isabel's blunt question.

"Oh, okay," Isabel said.

"Does that account for your fine collection of militaria, sir?" George asked, "because I do not believe you have experienced military service."

"That is correct on both counts, Mr Jenkins. I can see why you chose to become a detective. Now, would you like to see my collection that you returned to me? They are housed in the zoo at the far side of the estate."

I was tempted to make myself visible and tell this man to release all the creatures and ask him if he would like to be imprisoned in a cage. Jessie must have sensed this because telepathically she told me to say nothing. I said nothing but I left a parting gift for the millionaire by peeing on his expensive carpet. My, how that would stink in a while.

Bill moved things on before I disgraced myself (apart from peeing on carpets) by informing Rothschild we still had many loose ends to tie up.

With farewells and words of gratitude exchanged, we departed the warm study and continued our quest by Bill driving us back to Scotland Yard.

LATER THE SAME DAY

Bill Roberts conducted a thorough debriefing with all the team covering all the loose ends in the investigations into the catnapping caper and the exotic creatures gang. "Isabel let's start with you. What did you find out about Lady Josephine Ashford-Sinclair? If you recall, team, she reported her prized Siamese that was snatched in broad daylight from her Mayfair townhouse."

"I found out where the cook lived, she was the one who found the ransom note. I got chatty with her on her day off. She told me she thought the cat had never been stolen.

That ties in with what Kingsley said or rather didn't say when he was asked about this cat. He was surprised and had no idea what we were talking about if you recall."

"Yes, I do," George said, "and I also remember that rather suspicious answer given by Lady Ashford-Sinclair picked up by Isabel when Her Ladyship ignored the part of the question about anyone wishing *her harm.*"

"Exactly, so I spoke with a friend of the cook's who told me Ashford-Sinclair had been engaged in a long-running feud over some land with a Mayfair racketeer called Marmaduke Baldry. Clearly, he might have wanted to harm Her Ladyship," Isabel said.

"This is excellent detective work, Isabel, but it doesn't tell us if the cat was stolen or not," Bill said.

"I was just coming to that... you see one day last week I followed our Lady Josephine Ashford-Sinclair and she led me to her cousin's house in Pimlico. I waited until Her Ladyship had left then spoke with her cousin. She confirmed she was looking after the supposedly stolen cat whilst Her Ladyship's townhouse was being redecorated which we know was a lie," Isabel said.

"My goodness, that is brilliant work," Jessie said. "Do we know why she made the false report?"

"Piecing together what I was told by the cook and Her Ladyship's sister, Ashford-Sinclair cannot abide to be outside of the social gossip of the day so... it's clear to me she invented the theft just so she could be one of the tight circle of wealthy socialites grieving the loss of their prized cats," Isabel added with pride.

"Elementary, dear Watson," I said with yet another swish of my tail.

"Nothing elementary about it, Khan or should it be Holmes?" Jessie said.

"I agree, that was a great piece of detective work," Bill said.

"Sheesh... I'm only kidding. Lighten up you lot," I said.

"Look what you have done now," George said, "his feelings are hurt."

"Feelings, schmeelings," Bill said with a grin.

"Oi! That's my line, I'll have you know," I purred with a grin on my face.

The telephone rang interrupting the debriefing.

Chapter Fifteen

"Bill, it's Ward," came the voice from the other end—Inspector Clem Ward, to be precise. His tone was an odd blend of relief and urgency, like a man who'd just dodged an arrow only to find himself in a lion's den.

"Inspector, we heard you were on the run," Bill said, glancing at us with a puzzled expression.

"Indeed, but that's a tale for another time," Ward replied briskly. "I'm calling to commend you all on your remarkable work. The leads you've uncovered almost led you straight to the masterminds behind these criminal networks. I never doubted the Dale Street Agency and I'm sorry for duping you."

"Thank you, Inspector," Bill said, "we're just glad to help. Almost, you say. We arrested Kray as the leader of the catnappers and Edward Kingsley as the mastermind behind the theft of the exotic creatures and the auction. Is that right?"

"They were involved but the real brains behind it all was the Blackwell siblings—twins, operating under our noses the whole time. They had their fingers in both pies, so to speak. You'll get the full report soon. I made sure that the Commissioner puts a copy in your hands. Stay safe and keep up the sterling work."

With the call ended and Bill telling us the gist of Ward's message, Bill's face mirrored our collective shock. The notorious Blackwell twins had been a thorn in Scotland Yard's side for years. But now wasn't the time for dwelling on crime lords; we still had some loose ends.

The telephone rang again so Bill answered. He replaced the handset as quickly as he had picked it up.

"What is it, Bill? Why the serious face?" George said.

"Come, follow me. The Commissioner has summoned us to his office on the top floor."

"Me too?" I asked.

"Yes, but stay invisible, please and don't say a word," Bill said.

"Just as if..."

"Khan, no time for joking around," Jessie gently chided.

The Commissioner was seated behind a huge mahogany desk wearing his uniform decorated with what seemed to be a lot of scrambled eggs. I envisaged him wearing a cocked hat with a great feather plume like in one of those operettas but stifled the thought in case I broke Bill's rule.

The Commissioner cleared his throat. "Right, there is no other word to describe Detective Inspector Ward's actions. They were despicable and have brought shame on this great police force. He succumbed to temptation and assisted the catnapping ring in that he supplied them with information. He wasn't as involved in that gang as Detective Sergeant Kray."

"Sir, where is Ward now?" Bill said.

"He's in France."

"France, my goodness," Jessie said.

"Yes, he flew there in a private light aeroplane from a small air strip in rural Hampshire," the police chief said, "no doubt to evade arrest."

"He mentioned a report, sir, do you have a copy of it?" Bill said.

"I do. Peculiar thing is that Ward compiled this thorough report and asked that you be supplied with a copy," the man behind the desk said. "It seems like he is trying to make amends for his wrongdoings."

He handed a copy to Bill who swiftly flicked through its many pages. "Sir, it's clear to me I need to study this report then discuss it with the team and I need time to do that."

"I agree," the Commissioner said.

Two Hours Later – Bill's Office, Scotland Yard

"Okay, team, now that I have digested what Ward wrote in this report," Bill said waving the report in his hand, "it is the case that Kingsley was also a pawn and used as a respectable front man by the Blackwell twins, Reggie and Ronnie. What we didn't know is Kingsley was also Reginald Dawes. Kingsley was a master of disguise and that's how he got away with becoming Dawes. And it was Dawes or Kingsley, take your pick, who threatened to expose the socialites causing them to take their own lives."

"What had those wealthy individuals done then to make them kill themselves?" Isabel asked.

"Good question. They initially cooperated with Dawes' crooked schemes but then changed their minds. Rather than be shamed in their social circles, they sadly killed themselves," Bill said. "This was corroborated by Khan when he was undercover. Khan gave us some names of wealthy individuals who his feline friends said could be involved in the business of exotic creatures and some of them have died because they asked too many questions."

"So, my information was correct once more," I said with a flourish of my tail.

"True," Bill said, "and do you recall Mrs Winthrop who called Dawes a monster?

"I do," Jessie said, I can recall her very words 'Him... that Reginald Dawes. My husband was fine until he met Dawes and got involved with ruffians from the criminal underworld.'"

"George, you are quiet over there. Anything to say?" Bill said.

"Was there an overlap between the gangs? Did Ward cover that in his report?"

"That is an astute observation, George. There was with the Blackwells pulling the strings on both operations. Kingsley and Dawes, both the same person, were involved in both as were Ward and Kray to lesser extents as they were really pawns in the enterprise."

"I agree," I purred, "don't you recall overhearing one of the exotic gang talking about me. He said, 'talking animals like that black cat the copper told us about.'"

"Indeed, Khan, I do but what is so exotic about a gang?" Jessie smirked.

"They had exotic names like Fingers, Bulldog and Slick," I said with a straight face.

Jessie changed the topic. "So, do we arrest the Blackwell twins?" Jessie said.

"No, the Commissioner has sent a special task force to arrest them. A hand-picked team of detectives who are beyond suspicion," Bill said.

"And what about Ward?" I meowed.

"He will be arrested by the gendarmes and extradited back here to face the consequences of his actions," Bill said. "And they will also arrest Fingers, Bulldog, Slick and Tom Cobley."

"Who?" I said.

"It's a joke, Khan." Jessie said.

"How can it be a joke? It's not funny," I thought but that's humans for you.

"Right, team, our work here is done," George declared, clapping his hands together. "Let's head back to Liverpool."

"Back to Dale Street it is," I said, leading the way out. "Liverpool, our city of culture, cats, and... camaraderie."

"Cheers to that," Bill said, a broad smile on his face.

"Fish and chips await, my friends," I called over my shoulder, already anticipating the feast to come. And as we piled back into the train carriage at London's Euston station, I couldn't help but feel a sense of contentment. Another mystery solved, a new romance blooming, and the promise of future adventures. Indeed, life at the Dale Street Private Investigations Agency was anything but dull.

THE WARMTH OF CAMARADERIE enveloped the Dale Street office like a cozy blanket on a brisk late afternoon in Liverpool. Laughter ricocheted off the walls, mingling with the clinking of glasses and the rustle of fish and chips paper. I, Khan, lounged atop the filing cabinet, my green eyes flickering with mirth as I surveyed my companions.

"Did I ever tell you about the time I convinced a band of so-called 'ghost hunters' that the old manor was haunted by an aristocratic mouse?" I quipped, tail flicking in amusement.

"Go on then," Isabel chuckled, her interest piqued even as she dabbed malt vinegar onto her chips.

"Picture this," I began, voice rich with theatricality. "Midnight. Full moon. These ghost hunters with their silly gadgets prowling about the East Wing. I slipped into the grand piano and played a few high-pitched notes—"

"Mouse-like notes," George interjected, his moustache twitching in barely-contained glee.

"Exactly!" I purred. "They fled, screaming about the Phantom Rodent of Speke Hall. Took weeks before they dared to return."

"Brilliant!" Bill roared, slapping his knee. "You're a menace, Khan."

"Thank you," I said, feigning a humble bow. "I do try."

The laughter reached its peak, echoing through the room like a melody, and I leapt down to partake in the feast. But amidst the jovial spirit, I noticed something—a subtle exchange of glances between Jessie and George, a silent conversation that seemed to draw them away from the group.

"More tea, anyone?" Isabel offered, breaking the moment.

"Please," Jessie replied, slipping out of her chair. "I could use some fresh air."

"Mind if I join you?" George asked, rising to his feet with the aid of his cane.

"Of course not," Jessie said, a hint of something new, something tender, colouring her tone.

As the pair stepped into the cool afternoon, the office's atmosphere softened. The celebratory noise faded into the background, replaced by the gentle hum of the city outside.

"Jessie," George began. "This partnership—it's become something more, hasn't it?"

She paused, studying his earnest gaze. "It has," she admitted. "George, I—"

"Shh," he whispered, placing a finger on her lips. "No need for words. Our work speaks volumes. But there's another language we've yet to fully explore."

"Are you suggesting—?" Jessie's question trailed off, anticipation lacing her voice.

"Only if you're willing," George replied, reaching to take her hands in his. "To unravel this mystery together."

A smile touched Jessie's lips, bright as the stars above. "Then consider me your partner in crime... and perhaps, in life."

"Agreed," George murmured, his thumb brushing her knuckles gently.

"Let's promise, however our relationship unfolds, it won't interfere with our investigations," Jessie proposed, her practical nature taking over from the air of romance.

"Agreed," George echoed. "Our cases come first. But after hours..."

"Anything is possible," Jessie finished, her eyes reflecting the light of possibility.

"Absolutely anything," George affirmed, and in the quiet space between heartbeats, their partnership deepened into something richer, more profound.

Back inside, the laughter continued, stories flowed, and the echoes of triumph filled the room. Yet amidst it all, the unspoken bond between Jessie and George added a new layer to the tapestry of the Dale Street Private Investigations Agency—a touch of romance woven into the fabric of their shared destiny.

The clink of the letterbox snapped me from my contemplative gaze at the bustling street below. Jessie, ever alert, was already striding towards the door of our Dale Street office.

"Looks like we've got some late delivery post," she called over her shoulder.

"Let it not be another cursed chain letter," I murmured, padding softly behind her, my sleek black fur barely making a sound on the polished floorboards.

She chuckled, plucking the envelope from the mat. "It's from Scotland Yard."

"Ah, their penmanship does leave much to be desired," I quipped, peering up with interest as she tore open the seal.

"Listen to this," Jessie announced to the room, where George, Bill and Isabel were gathered, anticipation hanging in the air. "For exemplary service and dedication to resolving the catnapping and exotic creatures cases..."

"Get to the good part!" Khan interrupted, with a swift flick of his tail.

"Alright, Mr Impatient," Jessie laughed. "We are hereby commended for our outstanding contribution to the community."

A round of applause erupted and even George's reserved demeanour gave way to a broad smile that reached his sharp dark eyes. Isabel bounced with glee, clapping enthusiastically.

"Finally, some recognition that doesn't involve furballs," I said dryly, though the pride in my voice couldn't be disguised.

"Indeed," George agreed, leaning slightly on his cane. "We should frame this."

"Make sure it's hung at cat-eye level, so I can admire it daily," I insisted, eliciting a chuckle from the group.

"Look here," Isabel interjected, pointing at the newspaper she had been reading. The headline blared: 'Local Heroes Thwart Felonious Feline Fiends.' "We've made the news!"

"Can't say I'm surprised," I replied, whiskers twitching. "Journalists do love a good cat story."

"Especially one with such purr-fect resolution," Jessie added with a wink in my direction.

"Indeed," George said. "Each case we solve strengthens our reputation. We're one step closer to being the foremost private investigators in England."

"Speaking of which," Jessie said, turning to us, "we must remember who got us here—each other. I couldn't ask for a better team."

"Nor could I," George concurred. "Our combined efforts make us formidable."

"Here's to many more adventures," Bill raised an imaginary glass, his usual gruffness softened by the moment.

"Adventures that will undoubtedly require my unique expertise," I chimed in, "and perhaps a few well-timed naps."

"Always the modest one," Jessie teased, scratching behind my ears in that particularly delightful way.

"Modesty is for the ordinary," I purred contentedly. "And we, my dear friends, are anything but."

With laughter still ringing through the office, the team exchanged warm glances, each silently acknowledging the bond they'd formed. Outside, Liverpool continued its steady rhythm, unaware of the mysteries that awaited the Dale Street Private Investigations Agency.

But inside, hope and excitement filled the air, woven with threads of camaraderie and the promise of future enigmas. Together, Jessie, George, Bill, Isabel, and I stood ready to face whatever the supernatural world dared to throw our way.

"Tomorrow brings new opportunities," Jessie said.

"New mysteries to unravel," George added, his shrewd mind already turning.

"More chances to shine," Isabel chimed in, her enthusiasm undimmed.

"Let's not forget the inevitable glory," I remarked.

"Of course," Jessie grinned. "How could we ever overlook your glory, Khan?"

"Impossible," I stated matter-of-factly. "After all, every great team needs its legend."

"Sorry to mention more mundane matters," Isabel said.

"Don't be sorry, you are an important member of the investigation team now," Jessie said.

"Can my sister start permanently as the receptionist tomorrow?"

"Of course, tell Agnes to be in the office by eight thirty," Jessie said.

With that, we collectively turned our gazes toward the horizon, where the setting sun promised not just the end of a day, but the dawn of countless new adventures for the Dale Street Private Investigations Agency.

Chapter Sixteen

I WAS LAZILY SPRAWLED across the sunlit patch on the mahogany desk, my green eyes following the dance of dust motes in the air. With a stretch that seemed more for show than necessity, I yawned, revealing an impressive set of teeth.

"Quite the performance last night, wasn't it?" Jessie said, her voice tinged with both amusement and weariness as she leaned back in her chair, flicking through the case file one last time.

"Indeed," George concurred, tipping his homburg hat back slightly as he surveyed the room. "That spirit was rather more... tenacious than anticipated."

"Tenacious is one word for it," Jessie replied, her eyes meeting George's with a shared spark of triumph—and something else, something unspoken but palpably there.

"Ah, the new receptionist!" Isabel exclaimed, her voice cutting through the love-speak like a knife through butter. She gestured toward the door where her sister, a fresh-faced young woman with a beaming smile, stood. "Everyone, meet Agnes."

"Welcome to the Dale Street Private Investigations Agency, Agnes. Spirits, curses, and all manner of riddles—we solve them," Jessie declared, offering a warm, if somewhat mischievous, smile.

"Thank you, I'm thrilled to be here," Agnes said as she settled behind the reception desk, her eagerness almost tangible.

"Thrilled might be an overstatement once she meets our first ghost," George murmured under his breath, earning him a quick elbow nudge from Jessie and a chuckle from Isabel.

"Or once she realises the cat talks," Jessie whispered conspiratorially to George, her lips twitching in suppressed laughter.

"Hey, I'll have you know my conversations are often the highlight of the day," I interjected, feigning mock indignation as I opened one eye to regard them coolly. "You'd do well to remember that, Harper."

"Of course, Khan. How could we forget?" George replied, his dry wit surfacing as he gave the cat a playful wink.

"Let's hope Agnes has a good sense of humour," Jessie said, standing up to stretch her legs. "She'll need it around here."

"Speaking of humour," George started, leaning forward with a glint in his eye, "did I ever tell you about the time I convinced a whole group of tourists they had just missed the Loch Ness Monster by mere seconds?"

"Only every other week," Jessie teased, her eyes crinkling at the corners. She closed the distance between their desks, picking up a stray pen George had been looking for earlier. "Looking for this?"

"Perhaps," he conceded with a grateful nod, "but maybe I'm just enjoying the view."

"Cheeky," Jessie shot back but the warmth in her voice betrayed her true feelings.

Their banter was comfortably familiar, a dance they had perfected over countless cases. Yet now, each exchange seemed charged with the promise of something more, a thrilling possibility that neither dared to voice just yet.

"Isabel," Jessie called out, breaking the momentary silence, "why don't you give Agnes the grand tour? Including an introduction to our most eloquent feline member, of course."

"Right away," Isabel said with a grin, ushering her sister away from the front desk, leaving Jessie and George alone amidst the comfortable clutter of their office—their sanctuary against the unpredictable world of paranormal mysteries.

"Another case closed," George said softly, his voice carrying a note of contentment.

"Another mystery unravelled," Jessie added, her gaze lingering on George before shifting to the window, where the bustling streets of Liverpool reminded them of the endless possibilities that awaited.

"Shall we see what tomorrow brings, Miss Harper?" George asked, his dark eyes holding hers in a gentle challenge.

"Let's," Jessie agreed, her smile reflecting a shared anticipation of adventures yet to come—both professional and, perhaps, personal.

I leapt onto the desk with all the grace of a panther, though my eyes twinkled with the mischief of a streetwise tomcat. I looked at Jessie and George with bemusement as they sat opposite each other, an air of seriousness settling around them like a shroud.

"Blimey, you two look like someone's pinched your last sardine," I said breaking the tension as I swished my tail. "What's got your whiskers in a twist?"

Jessie exchanged a glance with George before turning her attention to the cat. "We're just..." She hesitated, searching for the right words. "We're considering the future."

"Ah, future talk. That usually means there's something more niggling at you than just which case to pick next." I settled down, curling my paws under me. "Spill it then."

George shifted, gripping his cane a little tighter. "It's complicated, Khan. We've been through quite the ordeal together, and it seems... it seems we've grown even closer."

"Close, eh? Like two books on a shelf, or more like a pair of gloves?" I said.

"More like two pieces of a puzzle," Jessie admitted, her voice barely above a whisper.

"Two pieces of a puzzle that are afraid to fit together, lest the picture becomes too permanent," George added, his analytical mind framing their dilemma perfectly.

"Look here, G.J., Jessie," I said, suddenly serious. "I've seen how you work together, and it's clear as crystal that you're both sharper when the other's around. But what's this I hear about fear?"

"We're partners, Khan," Jessie said. "And friends. We don't want to risk..."

"Risk smisk," I interjected with a flick of my ear. "You're worried about mucking up the agency dynamic. I get it. But let me pose you a question: has fear ever stopped you from chasing down a ghost or catching criminal gangs?"

"No," they responded simultaneously, and this time the laughter came easier.

"Exactly!" I said with a note of triumph. "You both have a knack for solving the unsolvable. Imagine combining that with the power of a romantic connection. It's not just about trust in each other's detective skills—it's about trusting in the strength of what you have together."

"Romance and detection," George pondered aloud. "It's uncharted territory, but if anyone can navigate it, it's us."

"Indeed," Jessie agreed, her hazel eyes meeting George's dark gaze with longing. "Our partnership has always been our greatest asset. Perhaps it's time we explore every aspect of it."

"Explore away," I purred approvingly. "Just remember, the Dale Street Private Investigations Agency isn't just known for its paranormal expertise. It's known for its heart—and that's something you two have in spades."

"Thank you, Khan," Jessie said warmly. "For everything."

"Think nothing of it," I replied with a dismissive wave of my paw. "Now, enough of this sentimental tomfoolery. There are mysteries out there begging to be solved by the likes of you."

"And solve them we shall," George affirmed, standing up and offering Jessie his hand. "Together."

"Partners in crime-solving and in life," Jessie accepted his hand with a smile that spoke volumes.

As I watched the two humans—no, partners—in a moment of silent agreement, I felt a purr of satisfaction rumble in my chest. They were embarking on a new chapter, one filled with promise and the unmistakable scent of adventure.

"Alright, you lovebirds," I chided gently. "Let's not keep the spirits waiting. We've got a reputation to uphold, after all."

With that, the three of us—one cat and two detectives on the cusp of romance—looked ahead to the next enigma that awaited unique blend of supernatural sleuthing and personal synergy.

Later That Day

Jessie leaned against the edge of her desk, flipping through a slender file of potential cases. The lamplight cast a warm glow over the papers, illuminating snippets of mystery that beckoned like uncharted stars in the night sky.

"Looks like we won't be short on excitement," she remarked with an impish grin directed toward George, who was perusing his own stack of case files across the room.

"Indeed," he replied without looking up, "the question is which adventure do we embark on first? The haunted manor in Strawberry Fields or the spectral sightings along the Mersey?" "Haunted manor sounds tempting," Jessie mused, tapping a finger against her chin. "But something tells me the Mersey spirits might be a more... riveting challenge."

"Riveting or not, it's bound to keep us on our toes," George said, finally meeting her gaze with a knowing look that sent a thrill of anticipation down her spine.

"Exactly what we need—"

"Ahem," I coughed but with a voice as smooth as velvet and with a hint of mischief. "If I may interject, I think you're forgetting the most riveting case of all."

Jessie and George turned towards me as I sat perched on the windowsill.

"Khan," they chorused, surprised I was present.

"Forgive my tardiness," I began, leaping gracefully onto the desktop. "I was just reminiscing about a particularly amusing incident from one of our past escapades—the one involving that so-called psychic medium."

"Oh?" Jessie raised an eyebrow, leaning in with interest.

"Let's just say," I continued with a purr of delight, "that her 'spiritual guide' was less of an ethereal being and more of a disgruntled pigeon she'd befriended. Quite the communicator, that bird. Had us chasing phantom whispers until I spotted it roosting atop the chandelier."

George let out a chuckle, his moustache twitching with amusement. "That would explain the strange cooing noises during the séance."

"Indeed," I agreed, my tail flicking with pride. "Though I must admit, watching you attempt to interpret those coos as otherworldly messages was rather entertaining."

"Entertaining for you, perhaps," Jessie retorted with feigned annoyance, though her eyes sparkled with humour. "I'll have you know I've never been so relieved to see a pigeon in my life."

"Relieved is one word for it," George added, sharing a conspiratorial smile with Jessie. "I believe the phrase 'saved by a pigeon' now holds a special place in our agency's annals."

"Speaking of special places," I said, shifting my weight as if preparing to launch into another tale, "I'm quite certain our future cases will provide ample opportunities for new stories. And who knows? We might even solve a mystery or two along the way."

"Only a mystery or two, Khan?" Jessie teased, her laughter mingling with the soft hum of the office. "I think we can aim a tad higher than that."

"Ah, but of course," I conceded with a sly wink. "With our combined talents and an ever-growing list of enigmas, the sky's the limit."

"Quite right," George affirmed, standing up to join Jessie at her desk. "And with each case, we'll grow stronger—not just as detectives, but as partners in every sense of the word."

As the evening wore on, the cozy office of the Dale Street Private Investigations Agency buzzed with the promise of adventure. Laughter echoed off the walls, carrying with it the unspoken agreement that whatever the future held, they would face it together—with a little help from Isabel, Bill and their feline friend, of course.

I decided it was an evening for telling tales so as I stretched languidly across the mahogany desk, my sleek black fur catching the warm glow of the lamplight. "You know," I began in my calm and measured tone with mischief in my eyes, "the spirits we encountered in that haunted bakery weren't just partial to poltergeist pranks. One had quite the penchant for puns."

Jessie leaned back in her chair looking perplexed. "Do tell," she said with a smile.

"Indeed," George chimed in from his spot by the bookshelf, thumbing through a tome on ancient curses. "I'm rather intrigued by the idea of a spectral stand-up comedian."

"Ah, well, during our little midnight escapade," I continued, "I overheard one particularly incorporeal fellow trying to lift the gloom. 'What do you get when you cross an angry spirit with a loaf of bread?' he howled. I almost chuckled despite the circumstances."

Jessie snorted, "And what is the punchline to this otherworldly joke?"

"Pure dead brilliant," George muttered under his breath, the corners of his mouth twitching.

"Boomerang baguettes," I said with impeccable timing. "They always come back for more!"

The room erupted with laughter, the tension built up from their recent London experiences dissipating into the evening air. As their chuckles subsided, Jessie's gaze met George's, a shared understanding passing between them.

"Laughter," Jessie mused, tucking a stray auburn lock behind her ear, "it really is our saving grace at times. With the darkness we face, it's vital, isn't it?"

"Absolutely," George agreed, leaning casually against the edge of Jessie's desk. "Without these moments of levity, the shadows might just become too much to bear."

They fell into a comfortable silence, each lost in thought. It was I who broke the stillness. "Fear has a way of filling the quiet spaces, does it not? But so does courage—and camaraderie."

"Speaking of fear," Jessie said, her voice softer now and vulnerable. "There are times, when the night is darkest, that I wonder if we're out of our depth, chasing these... these things beyond comprehension."

George nodded, a rare openness in his dark eyes. "I'd be lying if I said I didn't share those concerns. But then I remember who's by my side, and I find strength in that partnership."

"Partnership," Jessie echoed, casting a glance at George that lingered a touch too long, filled with unspoken promise.

"Indeed," George confirmed, his voice steady but imbued with warmth. "Our combined talents have seen us through many an enigma. And I dare say, there's no one else I'd rather have at my side, Jessie."

"Nor I, George." A faint blush coloured her cheeks.

I noted the exchange with a purr of contentment. The bond between Jessie and George was real, a connection that went beyond the professional. Though they were standing on the precipice of something new and uncertain, it was clear they were ready to take that leap—together.

"May your hearts be as courageous as your minds, dear friends," I intoned sagely. "For it is in vulnerability that true strength is found."

"Thank you, Khan," Jessie said, her smile genuine and grateful. "For everything."

"Always a pleasure," I replied with a dip of my head, the perfect picture of feline dignity.

As the conversation waned, Jessie and George shared one final look—a silent agreement that whatever lay ahead, humour, heart, and a hint of the extraordinary would see them through.

Jessie leaned back in her chair, the leather creaking under her weight. Across the desk, George's cane rested against the polished wood, a symbol of battles both past and ongoing. Between them sat stacks of files—cases closed and mysteries solved—a testament to their combined prowess.

"George," Jessie began, her voice carrying a new gravity, "whatever this... thing is between us, it can't get in the way of the agency. We've built something important here."

"Absolutely," George agreed, nodding solemnly. "Our work is paramount. But I believe we can navigate these waters. Together." His gaze held hers with an intensity that spoke volumes.

"Professionally and personally," she added, the corner of her mouth turning up ever so slightly. "We make quite the team, don't you think?"

"Indubitably," he chuckled. "I'd trust no one else to watch my back during a midnight séance or a stroll through the docks at night."

"Likewise. And if things get complicated..." Jessie let the sentence trail off, letting the unsaid 'we'll figure it out' hang in the air.

"Then we face it as we do everything else: head-on," George finished for her, his moustache twitching in a half-smile.

"Head-on," she repeated, a spark of mischief lighting up her face. "With a dash of humour, I hope."

"Speaking of humour," I interrupted, "did I ever tell you about the time I convinced the poltergeist haunting the old millinery shop that he was allergic to felt? Chaos, utter chaos!"

"Khan!" Jessie exclaimed, her tension easing at the interruption. "Only you could manage such a feat."

"Ah, but of course," I purred, leaping onto the desk with the grace only a cat—or rather, an enigmatic feline—could muster. "Humour, dear Jessie, is like a cat's ninth life; always there when you need it most."

"Thankfully, it seems we have endless supplies of both," George said, reaching over to give Khan an affectionate scratch behind the ears.

"Indeed, we do," Jessie agreed, her smile blossoming fully now. "And with that, I say we're ready for whatever comes next."

"Bring on the mysteries, the magic, and mayhem," I declared. "After all, what's life without a little whimsy?"

I perched atop the filing cabinet as I surveyed the room with an air of regal satisfaction. "I must say, I do enjoy the view from up here," I said casting a glance at Jessie and George, who had started to tidy up the office after a day's work.

"Is that so you can keep an eye on us or to ensure you don't miss out on any treats?" Jessie teased, stacking case files into a neat pile on her desk.

"Both," I said without missing a beat. "One must always be vigilant when it comes to snacks—and sneaky spectres."

George chuckled, the sound warm in the quiet of the office. "Well, we'd certainly be lost without your watchful eyes, Khan."

"Undeniably," I said with a flick of my ear. "But let's not forget my many other contributions. For instance, my unparalleled ability to sense when tea has reached the perfect sipping temperature."

"Ah, yes, the vital role of tea inspector," Jessie said, a playful glint in her eye as she moved to pour them all a cup. "We'd be steeped in trouble without you."

"Steeped in trouble?" George repeated with a smirk. "Really, Jessie?"

She shrugged, the corners of her mouth twitching with suppressed laughter. "What can I say? I've learned from the best."

"Touché," I said with a mock bow of my head.

Our banter filled the cozy office creating a warmth that seemed to seep into the very walls. The room was alive with the residue of the recent excitement—piles of research books haphazardly left open for quick reference, maps of Liverpool marked with pins and strings tracing investigative paths and the comforting scent of aged paper and polished wood.

It was a space that bore witness to triumphs and challenges, each object a testament to the cases we'd solved together—like the old typewriter that had once been used to forge spectral messages now serving as a reminder of their ingenuity.

"Imagine the stories this typewriter could tell," George said running a finger over its keys.

"Only if it doesn't jam halfway through," Jessie added, earning a chuckle from George.

"Ah, but even the most stubborn of machines cannot hinder our quest for truth and justice," I declared theatrically. "For we are the Dale Street Private Investigations Agency, purveyors of paranormal peace!"

"Hear, hear," Jessie raised her teacup in agreement, her laughter mingling with George's deeper tones.

"Cheers to that," George agreed, clinking his cup against hers.

The simple act felt like a seal over their newfound commitment—a promise to stand by each other both in the shadows of mystery and in the light of their affectionate camaraderie. It was a moment of pure contentment, set against the backdrop of their beloved agency, where the extraordinary was common and laughter was just as crucial as logic.

And as they sipped their tea among the relics of their shared victories, the two partners and I knew that whatever lay ahead, they would face it together—with wit, bravery, and the unbreakable bond of friendship.

I settled onto the windowsill—my usual pose when regaling company with tales. "So, I'm down by the docks, right? And this bloke thinks he can get away with smuggling cursed artefacts in a crate of bananas!"

"Bananas?" Jessie snorted, her eyes sparkling with mirth.

"Sure," I continued, "because nothing says 'unassuming cargo' like a bunch of bananas. Only, these had voodoo dolls nested among them. But did he reckon on our very own George here, with his knack for sniffing out the supernatural?"

"Apparently not," George chuckled, leaning closer to Jessie with a conspiratorial grin. "Though I'd say it was more luck than skill."

"Modesty, thy name is Jenkins," I quipped.

Their shared laughter echoed through the room, and there was a comfortable silence as we each reflected on the whirlwind of adventures that had brought us to this moment

A silence broken when Jessie said, "Here's to cracking more cases and... to whatever else the future holds." As she spoke her gaze lingered on George.

"Whatever else indeed," he replied, the promise in his voice wrapping around them like a comforting blanket.

Just as we settled into the quiet satisfaction of a job well done and the anticipation of what was to come, the door swung open with a sense of urgency that was all too familiar.

"Jessie, George, got a minute?" Bill Roberts stood framed in the doorway, the lines of his face etched with gravity that cut through the room's ease. He brushed a fleck of grey from his otherwise immaculate dark suit, his blue eyes scanning the office like beams from a lighthouse.

"Of course, Bill," Jessie replied, setting her teacup down with a delicate clink. "What's going on?"

"Something's come up," Bill began, his Welsh accent lending an even timbre to the urgency in his voice. "A case. Not your usual fare but one I think you'll want to hear about. It involves—"

"Wait, let me guess," I interjected unable to resist the pull of a good dramatic pause, "an ancient relic, a ghostly visage, or perhaps a cryptic curse?"

"Khan," George warned playfully, yet his eyes betrayed his curiosity.

Bill's lips twitched, betraying a smile. "Actually, it's a disappearance. A society lady vanished into thin air at her own gala last night. No signs of foul play, no ransom note, just gone... as if spirited away."

"Disappeared?" Jessie echoed, her brow furrowing. "That does sound like our kind of mystery."

"Indeed," Bill agreed, stepping fully into the office, his presence signalling the importance of the situation. "And I have a feeling this might be just the beginning."

"Sounds like we're in for another wild ride," George said, his hand finding Jessie's with subtle affection.

"Wild ride or not," I added, "we're ready for it. Aren't we?"

"Always," Jessie and George answered in unison, their hands clasped together—a symbol of unity in the face of the unknown.

As Bill unfolded the details of the new mystery, the spark of excitement ignited within us once again, promising that the next chapter for the Dale Street Private Investigations Agency would be filled with intrigue, danger, and a touch of the inexplicable.

"Right, everyone gather 'round," Jessie declared, her voice slicing through the thick anticipation that fogged the room. She stood at the head of their well-worn table, her eyes alight with the thrill of a fresh case.

I, Khan, still lounged on the windowsill, my tail flicking in sync with the pulsing energy of the room.

"Details, Bill. We need details," George pressed, leaning on his cane with one hand while his other rested casually on the worn leather of his chair. His moustache twitched in barely contained eagerness, a stark contrast to the usual composed detective.

"Of course," Bill obliged, laying out photographs and notes on the table. "Lady Ursula was last seen at her estate, near the gardens. No struggle, no screams. Guests were everywhere, yet nobody saw a thing."

"Sounds like she's quite the magician," I joked eliciting chuckles from Isabel and Agnes just outside the open door next to the receptionist desk. Even in these gravest of mysteries, humour was our unspoken language, a balm for the soul amidst the shadows we chased.

"Or perhaps it's us who will need to perform a disappearing act to uncover this one," Jessie mused, her gaze locked onto the images as if they held secrets only she could perceive.

"Disappearances are tricky," George noted with a thoughtful frown. "But not impossible. It takes a keen eye and—"

"—a dash of charm?" Jessie finished for him, their shared smile revealing more than their words ever could. The air between them crackled with something new, an invisible thread weaving itself into the fabric of their partnership.

"Indeed," George agreed, his dark eyes softening. "Just imagine the possibilities now that we're... exploring all angles."

"Exploring all angles," I echoed, rolling my eyes with feline sarcasm. "Is that what humans call it these days?"

Their laughter filled the room, a light-hearted interlude to the gravity of their task. They turned back to the evidence sprawled before them, their heads inching closer together as they discussed potential leads.

"Let's not forget," I said, leaping down to pad across the table, "our lady might have been spirited away by something less tangible than a kidnapper."

"Khan, always the supernatural sleuth," Isabel said, her voice carrying warmth as she joined us in the office with

Agnes in tow. "But he's right. We can't rule out any possibilities. By the way, sis, this is he who must not be mentioned outside of this company."

"Mention what? If I talked about a talking cat, I'd be committed," Agnes said.

"Correct," Jessie nodded. "But back to business. We'll start at the estate first thing tomorrow. See if we can pick up any... irregularities."

"Let's hope it's not another poltergeist with an attitude," I added, earning a round of amused looks. "They're terrible conversationalists."

"Alright, team," George announced, standing tall despite his reliance on the cane. "We've got our work cut out for us. But together, there's nothing we can't handle."

"Especially with our secret weapon," Jessie said, her eyes gleaming towards me.

"Flattery will get you everywhere, Harper," I replied, my green eyes sparkling with mischief.

The night had settled around Dale Street draping our office in comfortable shadows as we wrapped up our impromptu meeting. The cozy atmosphere of the room, with its familiar bookshelves and the comforting weight of history in every corner, grounded us.

"Tomorrow, we hit the ground running," Jessie said, gathering the photos and notes. "For now, rest up."

"Rest is for the weak," I stated grandly, though already contemplating the best spot for a nap.

"Or for those who don't have nine lives," George countered with a grin.

"Touché," I conceded, jumping off the table to claim my preferred cushion by the fireplace.

"Goodnight, you two," Isabel called out, casting one last look at Jessie and George who now seemed inseparable.

"Goodnight," Agnes said.

"Goodnight, Isabel, goodnight, Agnes," they replied in harmony, their voices blending together like a well-rehearsed duet.

"Goodnight, all," Bill said.

"Goodnight, Bill," Jessie and George replied as one voice.

As I left the office for the warm fire in the kitchen, the door closed behind me leaving the human detectives to their own devices, I couldn't help but feel a sense of contentment. Our little agency was blooming into something extraordinary, an amalgamation of talents, both ordinary and paranormal.

"Get some sleep, Khan," Jessie called after me, her tone laced with affection.

"Sleep? I'm nocturnal," I retorted without looking back, though I fully intended to curl up and drift into dreams of chasing spectral mice.

"Khan, don't let the bedbugs bite," George added, the laughter in his voice reaching my ears even as I sauntered away.

"Bedbugs? Please, I eat those for breakfast," I muttered under my breath. Yet as I settled into my cushion, the warmth of their presence lingered, and I couldn't deny the simple truth—I wouldn't trade this loveable ragtag bunch for all the catnip in England.

THE END

About the Author

KJ CORNWALL IS THE pen name of Stephen Bentley, a former British police Detective Sergeant, pioneering Operation Julie undercover detective, and barrister. He now writes in the true crime and crime fiction genres and contributes occasionally to Huffington Post UK on undercover policing, and mental health issues.

He is possibly best known for his bestselling Operation Julie memoir and as co-author of Operation George: A Gripping True Crime Story of an Audacious Undercover Sting.

His Operation Julie book has been optioned and is in development as an 8-part TV series in addition to that huge and unique police operation being pitched to broadcasters as a documentary. He is pleased that *Operation George* has also been optioned for the TV screen.

Stephen is a member of the UK's Society of Authors and the Crime Writers' Association.

With Dominic Smith, Stephen is a part of a writing team in the Undercover Legends series under the pen name of David Le Courageux.

Now a multi-genre author, Stephen also writes cozy mysteries in the pen name of KJ Cornwall.

You can listen to Stephen talking about his Operation Julie undercover days on the BBC Radio 4 Life Changing programme/podcast available 24/7 worldwide on BBC Sounds. And on the same platform, he also contributes to Acid Dream: The Great LSD Plot.

Sign up to the mailing list for news of books by Stephen and KJ Cornwall here[1].

---

1. Newsletter https://stephenbentley.eo.page/rz1db

Also By

<u>The publisher asks that you consider leaving a review of this book at the platform where you bought it. They do help!</u>

You can find all books written by Stephen Bentley and his pen names including KJ Cornwall using the Booklinker images below or viewing here.

You can also buy his books direct here.

KJ Cornwall Books2Read page is here. Stephen Bentley Books2Read page is here.

Visit the links by using the QR codes below for more details:

KHAN'S CLERKENWELL CATNAPPING CAPER 283

Jessie Harper Cozy Mystery Series

The Steve Regan Undercover Cop Thrillers

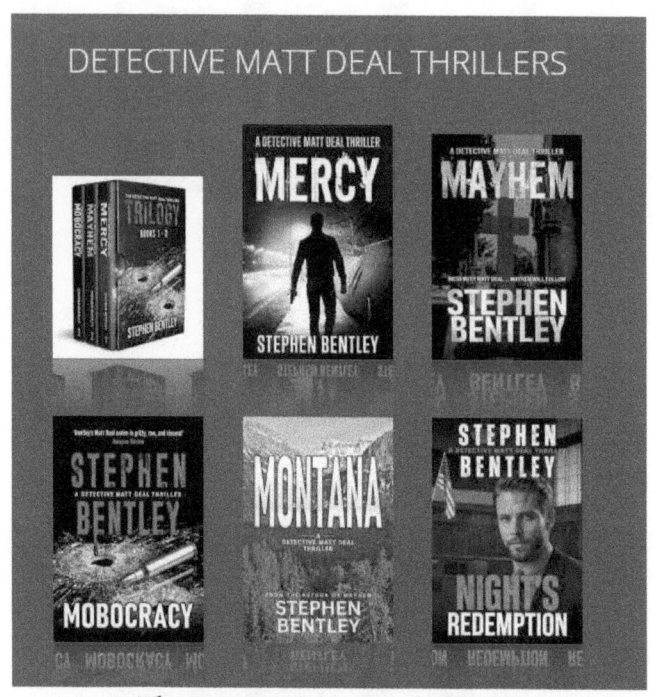

The Detective Matt Deal Thrillers

Bestselling True Crime

If you prefer to use QR codes you can find out more about all books written by KJ Cornwall and sign up for the mailing list by scanning the QR code below.

Similarly, you can find full details of true crime books and hard boiled thrillers written by Stephen Bentley by scanning the QR code below.

Acknowledgements

THIS BOOK MAY NOT have been possible without the immense help I received from Jane from England, Michele and Gabi from the United States, and Jacqui from France, who alpha and beta read the first drafts in addition to making further suggestions when it reached the ARC stage.

Heartfelt thanks are also owed to my Cozy Review team They did a sterling job and made life much easier for me and my editor. As usual, I also thank Esther, my editor, and my book cover designer, the lovely and talented Eeva who is the Book Khaleesi.

www.ingramcontent.com/pod-product-compliance
Ingram Content Group UK Ltd.
Pitfield, Milton Keynes, MK11 3LW, UK
UKHW042358301224
452994UK00001B/25